Stepping directly into her personal space, a sinful grin emerged across his ruggedly handsome face.

"I only ordered them to see you again. I could give a damn about cupcakes even though they're quite delicious. And you're right. I'm definitely coming back for more and *more* just to lay eyes on the breathtaking baker I can't stop thinking about." He traveled a gentle finger down her cheek and paused it on her lips, which parted on demand. "You are too tempting to resist."

Tiffani cursed inwardly at her mouth betraying her. Sucking in her breath, she stepped back, but when she did, all she felt was the wall next to the dessert table. His dark eyes held hers in a deep trance that could only be broken by a magical spell in a fairy-tale world far, far away.

He hadn't moved and neither had she. Even when the chef came into the room momentarily with a dish that smelled like roast beef and then exited as quickly as he'd come.

Before she could speak, Broderick yanked her body to his.

Dear Reader,

Tiffani Chase-Lake is one of my favorite heroines. I admire her ambition and strength to follow her dream of opening her own bakery, despite the fact she lost her husband at a young age and now has to raise her son without his father. Of course, she has a weakness: the suave business mogul, Broderick Hollingsworth.

When I created Tiffani, I wanted her to be unwavering in her decision to never marry again. However, she's all for an "in the moment" relationship because, well... a woman has needs, and she figures Broderick is the perfect man to fulfill them.

What she didn't factor in was that their first kiss was the sweetest kiss Broderick had ever experienced, and now he intends to make her his forever.

I hope you enjoy reading Tiffani and Broderick's sweet yet fiery romance. Feel free to contact me at candaceshaw.net.

Always,

Candace Shaw

The SWEETEST *Kiss*

CANDACE SHAW

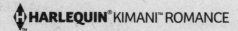

HARLEQUIN® KIMANI™ ROMANCE

Recycling programs
for this product may
not exist in your area.

ISBN-13: 978-0-373-86427-0

The Sweetest Kiss

Copyright © 2015 by Carmen S. Jones

For questions and comments about the quality of this book please contact us at CustomerService@Harlequin.com.

Printed in U.S.A.

JAN / /
2016

ⓗ HARLEQUIN®
™ www.Harlequin.com

Candace Shaw was born and raised under the sunny skies of northwest Florida and knew she wanted to become a writer after reading *Little Women* in fourth grade. After graduating from the University of West Florida with a degree in elementary education, Candace began teaching and put her dream of becoming a writer on hold, until one summer vacation she started writing again and hasn't stopped.

When Candace is not writing or researching for a book, she's reading, shopping, learning how to cook a new dish or spending time with her loving husband and their loyal, overprotective Weimaraner, Ali. She is currently working on her next fun, flirty and sexy romance novel.

You can contact Candace on her website at candaceshaw.net, on Facebook at facebook.com/authorcandaceshaw or you can Tweet her at twitter.com/candace_shaw.

Books by Candace Shaw

Harlequin Kimani Romance

Her Perfect Candidate
Journey to Seduction
The Sweetest Kiss

Visit the Author Profile page
at Harlequin.com for more titles.

Chapter 1

Glancing at his Rolex for the fifth time, Broderick Hollingsworth scanned the ballroom of the Pinnacle Boutique Hotel. White and purple roses overflowed from tall gold vases on the dinner tables as guests mingled, ate braised lamb and sipped on champagne while wearing their finest after-five attire. Weddings had never been his forte and he didn't even know why he'd RSVP'd to attend in the first place. He didn't necessarily consider himself a friend of the groom, who was his attorney and sometimes golf partner. Bryce Monroe apparently deemed him more than just a business associate, though, because the invite had stated it was an intimate affair for close family and friends. There were about one hundred and fifty or so people seated around twenty round tables waiting for the bride and groom to make their grand entrance as husband and wife. Everyone seemed to know everyone except him, but it didn't bother him. He saw a few familiar faces, all people he'd had business dealings with. He was somewhat of a loner at social events such as weddings and in life in general. However, he was seated at a table with another golf buddy and they'd made small talk while they waited.

Broderick needed to leave for another event, but his attention gravitated toward the bridal party seated at the front of the room. One of the bridesmaids he'd spotted during the ceremony had to be the most beautiful woman he'd ever laid eyes on. He'd noticed something elegant and classy about her as she'd glided like a graceful princess down the aisle. The memory of her clutchable hips swaying like a cool breeze in a fitted purple dress that hugged her tantalizing body like a glove was etched into his brain. He'd been so in awe of her during the ceremony that he hadn't realized it was over until he heard laughter and clapping around him. He'd stood to join in the cheers but never released his eyes from her delicate, beaming face.

Now Broderick was mesmerized once more as her flawless skin shimmered under the vast chandeliers of the ballroom. Her thick, waist-length hair was swept over her right shoulder in flowing curls showcasing her sculptured cheekbones on her alluring face. He did a customary glance of her left hand and was relieved to see no wedding ring. However, she was much too sexy and exquisite to not have a man in her life. He briefly perused the room but didn't notice anyone else staring in her direction. Some of the men were seated with their significant others. A few of the single ones he knew were cousins of the groom, but the other handful he wasn't sure about. Heck, for all he knew she could be dating his colleague next to him, though he doubted it.

Broderick continued watching her chat and laugh with one of the bridesmaids, not once realizing that he couldn't tear his gaze away. Even as his business associate conversed about the stock market rates of the day—which normally would have his full attention—he was focused on the breathtaking bridesmaid and her luscious lips. Lips like hers needed to be kissed and caressed gently at first to savor their warmth and to listen to her soft moans before crashing further into her mouth with fervor. Her moans would undoubtedly increase from the intensity of being under his command. He took a sip of his brandy while his thoughts carried him to a place of drawing her to him and tasting her divine, sweet mouth. His tongue lingered on the warmth of the liquor as he imagined doing the same to her succulent lips.

The wedding coordinator's announcement of the newlyweds entering the room jerked Broderick from his daydream as everyone stood and yelled as Bryce and his wife, Sydney, zoomed into the middle of the dance floor on a Harley. Broderick wasn't surprised—the newlyweds both loved motorcycles and owned several.

Once the excitement died down, he was tempted to stride over to the lovely woman who had filled his thoughts for the last hour. Unfortunately, a quick swipe of her cell phone from the table and a grimace on her adorable face had her slipping out of a side door in a flash.

He returned his attention to his colleague, who still yammered on about the stock market without realizing Broderick hadn't heard a single word.

"So are you considering taking your money out of Swanson Technologies?"

Broderick pondered for a moment and sipped the rest of his drink. "I'll have my stockbroker look over everything before making a decision. It's the weekend, Dave. Let's just enjoy the moment."

Dave scanned his face with puzzlement. "I don't think I've ever heard you say anything like that before. *Ever.*"

Grabbing his empty plate, Broderick shrugged and stood. "I don't talk about business all the time." He knew that was a lie. As a real estate developer and investor in Atlanta, making more millions was the only thought on his mind. He owned a lot of property in Georgia and the surrounding states, including a percentage of the hotel he was currently standing in. However, staring at the dazzling woman had clouded his brain. He quickly shrugged it off as he made his way to the dessert table, which was laden with tiers of assorted cupcakes. A woman like her would want more than just a fling.

She'd want a real relationship that would eventually lead to a ring on her dainty finger, an extravagant wedding, children and cross-country vacations in a Winnebago. Maybe even a dog. No, that wasn't on his agenda. At age thirty-seven, he knew he should consider settling down, though the thought irked him.

He reprimanded himself for even parading such ideas and reached out to grab a cupcake. Biting into it, he was impressed by the deliciousness of the caramel icing and took another bite.

"Mmm...this is delectable," he said out loud, setting it on his plate and reaching for another one.

"Why thank you."

A wicked grin lined his face as the angelic voice of a woman caressed his back like heat from the sun. Even though he'd never heard her speak before he knew it had to be the lady who'd caught his curiosity. He pivoted to stare, almost eye level with the tall, regal beauty who was even more intriguing up close. She wore a pleased smile that showcased a yummy dimple on her left cheek.

"You made these delicious cupcakes?"

She glanced at them before resting her cinnamon eyes on him once more. "Yes and the wedding cakes. The one you have is the same flavor as the groom's motorcycle-shaped cake. I'm glad you like it."

"Like is an understatement," he paused, stepping closer to her and lowering his voice. "I love it." He swished his tongue to the left corner of his mouth to lick off icing he felt.

He noted a slight gulp as she backed up a tad and turned toward the dessert table. "Well, there's plenty here for you to select from."

"Mmm…yeah, but I prefer the caramel one. It's quite mouthwatering."

Running her fingers through the top tresses of her hair, she tried to squash a smile while biting her bottom lip.

Goodness she was sexy, but he could sense there was so much more to her than that, and he wanted… no, needed to know.

"I'm Broderick Hollingsworth, and if I had to guess I'd say your name is Angel."

Releasing a cute giggle, she ran her fingers through her hair once more. "That's very sweet, Mr. Hollingsworth, but it's Tiffani Chase…umm Lake." She stumbled on her words and shook her head as if she'd forgotten. "It's hyphenated."

He glanced at her ringless left hand. "You're married?" he asked with disappointment, hoping that her husband wasn't somewhere nearby watching their interaction and feeling ready to fight. Not that Broderick was scared. At six-feet-three inches and two hundred and ten pounds of all muscle, he feared no one; however, he would never disrespect anyone's marriage. He decided to back up a few steps.

She waved her hands back and forth. "Oh…no…not anymore. My husband died a little over three years ago."

"I'm so sorry to hear that," he said, trying to sound

as sincere as possible while moving to his original spot in front of her. A server with a tray of champagne flutes approached. Broderick took two and handed one to Tiffani.

Sipping the champagne, a faraway expression washed over her features. "Thank you. My family and friends have been a huge support. Plus, I have to stay strong and focused for my son, Keith Jr. He's my only concern."

Son? He had a rule to never date women with children, especially young children. He was spontaneous and didn't want to deal with the hassle of a woman trying to secure a babysitter at the last minute or having to be back by a certain time. Then there were the other issues like she couldn't spend the night at his house or he couldn't stay over at hers. Or dealing with the fathers or meeting the child, who may or may not like him. However, there was something intriguing about Tiffani that had piqued his curiosity, and there were exceptions to every rule, especially those he made.

"How old is he?"

"KJ is eight. He was the ring bearer in the wedding."

"Ah, I remembered him coming down the aisle, looking quite dapper in his tux." Broderick glanced around the room. "Where is he?"

"Oh, I sent him home with the babysitter after the ceremony. I'll be here late and didn't want him up past his bedtime."

"Makes sense. So, is baking a hobby for you?"

"At first. Now I own a bakery in the Dunwoody area. Cupcakes are my specialty, but I can make just about any dessert." Setting the flute on the table, she opened her evening clutch and pulled out a sterling-silver business card case engraved with her initials. "Here's my card."

His hand brushed her dainty, French-manicured one as he took the pink card from her. Her skin was warm and he had the urge to travel his fingers along the rest of her. He cleared his throat and read the card before he acted on his thoughts.

"Sweet Treats." Broderick pondered for a moment as he noticed the bride's twin sister, who was also his interior decorator, wave in their direction. Apparently Tiffani was needed for something as she nodded and held up a finger to signal she'd be there in a moment.

"Before you go, I'm having a get-together for some business associates at my home next week. Can you make some of these delicious cupcakes for me?"

"Why, of course. My information is on the card including my website, which has a list of desserts and prices."

"Great. I'll have my secretary call you on Monday."

Her face scrunched for a second but perked back up. Was she disappointed that he wouldn't be the one calling? Making arrangements for events wasn't something he typically did, but a jab pierced his heart for a moment when her lovely face saddened.

"I'm closed on Sunday and Mondays, but I'll be there

Monday morning preparing for an order." She looked past him once more. "I have to go. It was a pleasure meeting you, Mr. Hollingsworth." She rushed off before he could say goodbye. He watched her and the other bridesmaids hurry through the main entrance.

His cell phone vibrated in his pocket. Retrieving it, he read the text message on the screen. It was his business manager, Josh Powell reminding him of the networking social he was supposed to be attending that very moment. His intention had been to leave after the wedding ceremony, but that was before he'd laid eyes on Tiffani and wanted to see her once more. Luckily, the other event was only a few blocks up on Peachtree Road in the Buckhead district, and he sent a message back that he would be there in twenty minutes.

Broderick bid his goodbyes to the newlyweds and thanked them for inviting him. As he walked out of the ballroom, he spotted Tiffani heading back inside. He caught her eyes as she graced him with the sweetest smile a woman had given him since his mother had died. He put a little more pep in his step as he trekked to the valet stand. He knew he had to see Tiffani and her breathtaking smile again.

"So I noticed you were having an in-depth conversation with Broderick Hollingsworth. I almost hated to interrupt you," Megan Chase-Monroe stated as she and Tiffani headed back to their seats at the bridal party table. "Is there a date in the near future? That was some smile you gave him."

Plopping into a purple tulle-covered chair, Tiffani glanced at her baby cousin out the corner of her eye. "No. No date. He wants to order cupcakes for an event he's having. That's all."

Megan scrunched her forehead and frowned. "Cupcakes for an event? Broderick is the last man on Earth who would care about ordering anything. He's one of those millionaires who has a ton of staff at his beck and call. He's sort of standoffish and serious most of the time. Everything is business with him. Perhaps he wanted your number, hence the ordering of the cupcakes," she stated with a beaming face. Megan was the hopeless romantic of the family and wanted everyone to be in love and happy.

"He was definitely flirting with me but he was pleasant." *And so sexy*, she added in her head. "He said his secretary would call. How do you know him?"

"He's a real estate developer and investor. I've decorated a plethora of projects for him including his mansion and beach home."

Tiffani nodded and tried to keep her focus on the bride and groom's first dance, but her thoughts drifted back to the man whose charming smile nearly knocked her over when he turned around. She wasn't expecting a handsome man with a commanding demeanor who outshined every other male in the room. He had a yummy, smooth, butterscotch-toned face with a neatly trimmed beard and mustache that surrounded his sexy lips. He'd had a little icing on the corner of his mouth and she'd had to restrain herself from reaching over and wiping it off…with her tongue. When he'd swished his tongue over, she'd nearly melted in a steaming puddle at his feet.

She couldn't believe her thought process. Sure, she'd oohed and aahed over men, but they were famous men on the movie screen like Denzel Washington or George Clooney. Never in person to the point of blushing. Tiffani was almost certain her cheeks had turned a rosy pink, and more than likely he'd noticed. She was disappointed when she saw him leave and had hoped perhaps he was just stepping out for a moment. However, she'd glanced over her shoulder before going back into the ballroom to see him handing a slip to the valet.

"Can you believe Sydney actually changed out of her wedding dress and into a white leather jacket and pants?" Megan asked. "I had no idea she was going to do that."

Megan's question jolted Tiffani from her thoughts, and she was grateful. Daydreaming about a man she would never see again wasn't on her agenda. No need in getting all hot and bothered for nothing. If he'd wanted to ask her out he would've. Apparently he wasn't interested. Not that she was, but there was a mystery about him she found intriguing, especially now that she'd learned from Megan he was standoffish. He hadn't exhibited that. Her experience with him had been quite the opposite.

"I don't know why you're surprised. Your twin zoomed in here on the back of a Harley. At least she still wore her veil and had her bouquet."

"Almost time for the bouquet toss," Megan sung in an upbeat manner.

Here we go again, Tiffani thought. At age thirty-two, she wasn't in the mindset to concern herself with catching bouquets. Yes, she was single but, considering she never wanted to marry again, there wasn't any point in rushing to the dance floor. Especially with a bunch of women who had the preconceived fairy-tale notion that they would be the next to marry if they were lucky enough to catch the bouquet.

"I'll let the young single ladies who really want to get married claw over a bunch of roses."

"Tiff, you're still young. I know you continue to say that you don't want to ever marry again, though you never know. You remember when Raven confided in us after her husband died that she was done with marriage? Well, now she's happily married again. It can happen. You never know what is in store for you."

Tiffani gazed out onto the floor as her cousin Raven Arrington-Phillips and her husband, Armand, danced. The DJ had just instructed that everyone join the bride and groom for the Electric Slide. True, her cousin had found love again after losing her husband, but their situations were completely different. Raven had been devastatingly heartbroken and never thought she could love again.

Annoyed with the topic, Tiffani sighed and turned toward Megan. "You know the real reason why I've decided not to, so let's just drop it."

Megan nodded and patted Tiffani's hand. "Okay, end of discussion."

Satisfied with her cousin's answer, Tiffani excused herself to make sure everything was set for the cake cuttings. She already knew it was because she'd checked just before she had met Broderick, but she needed a moment alone. Being reminded of her marriage from hell was always a sore subject.

Later on that night, the conversation with Megan still lingered in Tiffani's mind when she kissed her son's forehead as he slept. Tiffani knew she meant well, but Megan wasn't the one who had been married to a controlling as well as verbally and mentally abusive man. The thought of having to live through that again wasn't a life she desired. She was at peace and happier than she'd been in a long time. Plus, the fact that a handsome man had flirted with her that evening reminded her that men still found her attractive. Although she never wanted to remarry, she wasn't closed off from dating.

Retreating to her bedroom, she grabbed her laptop from under the bed and posted a few pictures she'd taken at the wedding and some selfies with KJ to her blog "My New Life." She'd started it a year after her husband had passed. At first, the majority of her posts centered around fun yet inexpensive activities to do with children, hands-on lesson plans for elementary school teachers, how to save on grocery shopping and healthy recipes for the single mother. Once she'd stopped teaching third grade and opened her bakery five months ago, Tiffani began to discuss her transition into the small business world while still maintaining a structured balance for her son.

She smiled with pride at the huge grin on KJ's face that matched hers before pressing Send. Shutting off the laptop, Tiffani set it on the nightstand next to the purple and white roses she'd carried in the wedding. Broderick Hollingsworth's handsome face appeared in her mind. She shook her head with a smirk as she reached out to turn off the bedside lamp and slid under her down comforter. Laughing, she realized how ridiculous she was behaving over a man who probably hadn't given her a second thought.

Chapter 2

Broderick tossed his jacket and tie on the chaise lounge in front of his bed before he strode through to the adjoining cherrywood-paneled study. Leaning over his desk, he flicked on the lamp and turned on his laptop. Pulling out his wallet, he flipped through all of the cards he'd received that night both at the wedding and the business mixer until he found the only one he cared about. The rest of them would go to Josh or his secretary for possible meetings.

Retreating to the wet bar, Broderick poured a scotch while his computer started. Once settled in his black leather swivel chair, he typed in the website on the pink card and sipped his drink as the Sweet Treats website loaded. Like Tiffani's personality, it was whimsical and girly with bright colors. A smooth jazz tune played in the background and a variety of cupcakes scrolled on the banner. He glanced at the tabs on the search bar, but the one titled "About the Baker" caught his eye. Considering he already knew what he was going to order, he figured he could look at desserts later. Right now, he wanted to know more about the sexy baker he'd found utterly intriguing. Clicking on the tab, he was elated to see an adorable picture of Tiffani wearing a pink chef's jacket with a matching chef's hat while holding a tray of cupcakes. He skimmed over her biography. It discussed her baking experience and expertise but didn't mention anything personal about her. At the end of the short paragraph, a link titled "My New Life" grabbed his attention and he hoped it would lead to more information about Tiffani.

"Bingo," he said, sipping his scotch as he scrolled through the posts that had begun more than two years ago.

She seemed to post about once or twice a month. Most of them were centered on her son, gardening, recipes and her transition from teaching to opening her bakery five months ago.

Broderick was impressed with her passion for her business but always making sure to put her son first. On one of the blog posts, she'd discussed her daily routine of dropping KJ off to school at seven, heading to the bakery by eight, then baking and preparing nonstop until the shop opened at ten. Her assistant would arrive at nine and stayed until they closed at five. Tiffani or one of her parents, who were retired, would pick up KJ from school and bring him to the bakery, where he would do homework. They would leave around six and head home unless he had karate or swim lessons. Any time after work was spent with him until his bedtime, after which she'd stay up to bake special orders for the next day.

Broderick's thoughts blasted him back to his childhood. Although his mother had loved him, she'd loved drugs and men as well. After she died of an overdose at a crack house when he was eight years old, he found himself bouncing around between different relatives or foster homes until he was eighteen. Glancing at a picture on his desk of his mother and himself during one of her good days, he sighed and shook his head to brush away the hurtful memories. He clicked back to the first page of Tiffani's blog and was pleasantly surprised to see a new post had uploaded moments before. It was a short write-up about the wedding and a couple of selfies of her and KJ making goofy faces in a mirror. Clicking on the picture, Broderick zoomed in until he only saw Tiffani. Even making fish lips and crossing her eyes, she was still breathtakingly beautiful.

He perused over her website quickly, taking note of the different desserts Sweet Treats offered. Even though the only sweet treat he desired wasn't on the menu, he was determined to savor it.

The ringing of Tiffani's cell phone in her apron pocket disrupted her concentration in icing the tops of the German chocolate cupcakes for an order later on that day. Placing the icing bag on the prep station counter, she hurriedly answered the phone before it went to voice mail.

"Hello, Sweet Treats. This is Tiffani. How may I assist you?" she asked in a fake chipper voice. It was eight o'clock on a Monday morning and she really needed coffee. A pot was brewing and she'd been waiting impatiently for the beep to signify it was ready.

"Good morning, Tiffani. This is Broderick Hollingsworth. How are you?"

The sexy, baritone voice in her ear rippled a warm shiver through her veins. Breath escaped her windpipes and floated out into the kitchen of her bakery. He was the last person she was expecting a call from.

She cleared her throat and hoped when she opened her mouth, her words didn't sound like gibberish.

"Hi, Mr. Hollingsworth. I'm well. What can I do for you?" she asked calmly even though butterflies swirled in her stomach.

"I wanted to place an order for a few dozen cupcakes. Is this a good time?"

Didn't Megan say that isn't his type of thing to do?

"Of course. Just give me a moment to grab my laptop." *And to grab some ice water.* No matter what he said, his deep seductive tone was present. She knew it wasn't on purpose. That was just how he spoke. Nonetheless, a scorching current rushed through every cell of her body every time he uttered a word. She didn't know how she was going to concentrate on placing his order with his voice so close, as if he were really present in her shop.

"Is it okay if I stop by instead?"

Stop by? Her face flushed with heat at the notion of him striding in wearing a custom-made suit similar to the one he'd worn to the wedding—one that enhanced his manly physique. Her heart hammered rapidly against her chest and her skin crawled with anticipation. She wasn't sure if she could handle being graced with his overbearing presence in her cozy bakery. *Alone.*

"Um…sure you can stop by." She picked up the icing bag once more to finish the last cupcake from that batch. There were two dozen more cooling on an adjacent prep station that needed to be done by noon.

"I'll be there soon."

"Okay…" She stopped abruptly as the chime of the doorbell sounded and her pulse raced. "Um…oh you meant *really* soon."

"I just rang the bell," he stated matter-of-factly in a low, deep tone that was becoming nerve-racking in her ear.

"I'll be out front in a moment." She pressed the end button on her phone just as the coffeemaker beeped. However, she no longer needed it. The fact that Broderick was there had awakened her and also flustered her more than she cared to admit to herself.

Untying the apron from around her waist, she

glanced down at her black velour jogging suit that had flour on the front of the jacket. She wiped it off with her hand but ended up making more of a mess. She took it off and flung it over a bar stool at the prep counter. Then she pushed the kitchen door open and stared straight into the eyes of Broderick, who stood on the other side of the glass door on the sidewalk about a hundred feet away. She'd been correct in her assumption that he would be strikingly dashing in a suit that did nothing to hide his fine, muscular body. The waves of his low cut, jet-black hair and freshly shaven beard gave him a ready-for-the-camera edge.

As Tiffani neared the front door, she noticed her reflection in the glass and panicked. In her haste to let him in from the October morning chill, she'd forgotten she was wearing a hairnet over a messy ponytail. A scrumptious man stood outside her shop and she looked a hot mess. Dang, she could have at least appeared somewhat presentable. Not only that, she wasn't wearing a bra under her pink tank top.

Taking a deep breath, she unlocked the door and hoped the cool air wouldn't place her nipples on display.

"Good morning," he said, passing through as she stood to the side and out of the way of the wind that rushed in along with his enticing scent.

I was right, Tiffani thought as she closed and locked the door. His presence in her little bakery was indeed overpowering and commanding. This man belonged in a boardroom on the top floor of a skyscraper conducting meetings on how to make more millions, not ordering cupcakes from a place probably smaller than his bathroom.

His eyes perused the shop for a moment before settling back on her. "Beautiful. Very beautiful, indeed. Reminds me of you." He gazed around again, this time nodding his head as if he were an inspector.

Tiffani barely stammered out a meek "thank you" while glancing around as well, as if for the first time. Hot pink walls that displayed blown-up pictures of desserts she'd made and turquoise drapes flanked either side of the glass wall at the front of the shop. On one side of the door was a booth decorated with an array of pastel toss pillows and on the other side, a window seat. A bookshelf on the adjoining wall housed classic children's books and some of her favorite Harlequin romance novels. On the same wall was a long counter with a glass display that was empty at the moment, but it usually contained cupcakes, pastries and other treats. On the opposite side, eight wrought-iron bistro tables with three chairs each lined the wall. She'd wanted the atmosphere classy and inviting and thanks to Megan it was.

"Did I catch you at a bad time?" he asked, glimpsing at her hairnet.

Geez. He looked at the hairnet. "No. Just baking as usual. You can have a seat, and I'll grab my laptop."

She hurried into the kitchen and straight back to her office as her heart raced. Men never made her nervous, so she didn't know why Broderick's presence was driving her insane. Who was she kidding? She knew why. He was gorgeous, intriguing and downright sexy. Plus, she'd daydreamed about him so much yesterday that she'd burned a batch of chocolate chip and macadamia nut cookies that KJ had requested for his teacher's birthday.

Tossing the hairnet on her desk, she removed the hairband and shook her curls loose around her shoulders. Exhaling, she grabbed her laptop and headed out to rejoin Broderick. When she returned, his eyes caught hers and an amused smile crossed his face as she sat in the chair in front of him.

"So how many people are going to be at your party and when is it?" she asked in her most professional tone while opening her laptop to begin filling out the form.

"About twenty to thirty and it's Thursday at 7:00 in the evening at my home."

"So you need about three dozen cupcakes or was there another dessert you wanted?"

A cocky grin inched up his right jawline, and he met her eyes in a heated gaze. She gulped as her breath caught in her throat. His hazy, seductive expression admitted he'd heard her words in a completely different way. She froze, waiting for an answer.

He leaned in toward her. "As a matter fact there is something else I want," he paused as his stare turned serious.

"What?" she asked barely above a whisper. She held

her body as still as possible to suppress possible shudders that resulted from the fear of him replying "you" as a response to what he wanted.

"Your sweet potato pie."

Surely she'd misheard him.

"Huh?"

"I read over the list of other desserts you make, and I'd love to taste your sweet potato pie."

"Oh…sure…of course. How many?" she asked, attempting to keep her voice steady.

"Just one. It's for me."

Relieved that he wasn't referring to her, Tiffani's heartbeat slowed to a normal pace—or as normal as possible with him sitting there eyeing her like a hungry animal. "Okay, I'll add that to your order." She kept her eyes downcast on the computer screen. She could no longer meet his penetrating gaze. However, she had kind of hoped he was going to say "you." "You want a variety like at the wedding?"

"Yes, that's fine. I saw on your website that you also deliver for an extra fee."

"Yes, one of my employees can deliver and set up around six o'clock. Does that time work for you?"

"Um…sure," he shrugged.

They spent the next few minutes finishing up his order. She suddenly felt disappointed because she figured he'd soon be leaving. Closing her laptop, she folded her hands on the table. He seemed to be a really nice guy, and he wasn't standoffish at all. Perhaps Megan had been wrong.

"Thank you so much for ordering cupcakes for your get-together."

"You're welcome. I like to help out small business owners…especially ones as beautiful as you."

"Mr. Hollingsworth…" Her face flushed with heat.

"No, call me Broderick. And I meant what I said. You're a beautiful woman. Can I share something with you?"

"Sure."

"I don't usually order food and whatnot for my events. My secretary or my housekeeper takes care of such things, but I wanted to see you and your sweet smile again."

She couldn't help but smile wide followed by a giggle.

"Yep, that's the one."

Oh my goodness. I'm acting like a silly teenager with her first crush.

She cleared her throat. "Thank you. You're very sweet."

Broderick snickered. "Sweet? I've been called a lot of things, my dear, but sweet isn't one of them."

Tiffani managed to stifle a gulp as his piercing stare raked over her bare neck and shoulders and down to the top of her cleavage. Heat rose in her cheeks at his perusal of her, and she felt her nipples hardening and pushing on her shirt. She realized she needed to change the subject and quick, especially when he bit his lower lip before resting his mesmerizing eyes back on her face.

Running her fingers through her hair, they landed on both sides of her shoulders and down her shirt in an attempt to cover her breasts. She caught him raise a wicked eyebrow at her gesture. She sensed he was about to speak but she cut him off.

"So why did you decide on sweet potato pie? Is that something your mother or grandmother makes?"

The seductive expression he'd worn changed into a sullen frown. He looked away from her for a moment, and when he rested his eyes on her again she noticed sadness.

"No, nothing like that. Just wanted to try it since it's listed as being a seasonal item because of the upcoming holidays," he stated as upbeat as possible. He stood and swiped his cell phone off of the table. "I have a meeting at my office soon."

She stood as well, feeling guilty that he'd shut down when she'd asked about his family. Maybe his mother or grandmother or even both had died. Maybe it was recent.

"Before you go, I have something for you." She rushed back into the kitchen and placed half a dozen pecan apple bear claws she'd made for the next day into a box for him. Tiffani felt awful and wanted to make it up to him somehow. She closed the yellow-and-white striped box that matched the awning on the bakery and headed to the front. He was standing next to the door scrolling through his cell phone with a strained expression.

Handing him the box, she smiled warmly, hoping it would take him out of whatever mood he was now in. The mood she'd caused. "I hope you like bear claws. Freshly made this morning."

His pleasant demeanor from earlier returned as his face softened. "Thank you," he said in a sincere tone. "I love sweet things, but you already know that, don't you?" He winked and reached for the door. "I'll eat one on the way to work."

"I'd prefer you drive safely instead."

"I'm not driving," he answered, pushing the door open and nodding his head toward a black Bentley and a man dressed in a black suit, who opened the back door as Broderick approached. Glancing over his shoulder, his eyes briefly traveled over her. "Have a great day, beautiful."

"You, too."

Once Tiffani settled back in the kitchen, she finally exhaled.

Chapter 3

Tiffani drove up to the wrought-iron gate of a vast mansion in the West Paces Ferry area suburb of Atlanta. She spotted an intercom panel, rolled down her window and pressed the button. While she waited for a response, she focused on the massive brown brick and stone house in front of her—well, a half of a mile away it seemed down the long driveway that matched the brick on the house. Today's plans hadn't included dropping the cupcakes off at Broderick's home, but her assistant, Kendall, had a study group that evening for a midterm exam. Luckily, it was grandparents' day at KJ's school, so he could go home with them. Still waiting for an answer, she pushed the button again. She was starting to get antsy because she was already fifteen minutes late thanks to traffic and making a wrong turn. She knew it wouldn't take her more than twenty minutes to set the cupcakes on the serving platters that Matilda, Broderick's housekeeper, promised would already be placed on the dessert table. She'd called that morning to verify the set-up time and to inform Tiffani that there was no need to bring any serving platters because she would be providing crystal ones.

The gate opened and a lady's voice from the intercom stated to drive around to the side door by the garage. Once at the side entrance, Tiffani gathered the container with the cupcakes and the pie from the backseat. She was greeted with a warm smile from a middle-aged woman dressed in the standard black-and-white maid's uniform.

"Hello, I'm Matilda. Do you need help bringing anything in?"

"Nice to meet you and no I don't. Thank you." She followed Matilda through the mudroom and into a huge gourmet kitchen where a chef and his crew were busy preparing food. Delicious aromas filled the atmosphere and it reminded Tiffani that she hadn't eaten since lunch.

As they continued to the dining room, Tiffani noticed Megan's expertise everywhere, from the heavy amethyst drapes that flowed from the top of the ceiling down to the walnut hardwood floors. The exquisite, long dining room table that sat at least twenty was surrounded by gold upholstered chairs. Bouquets of calla lilies were spread out on the table that was laden with serving trays and bowls.

"You can set up the cupcakes here, Ms. Lake." Matilda waved her hands toward a buffet table on the wall that had two square crystal platters.

"These are gorgeous…almost too gorgeous for my cupcakes."

"I'm sure they will look splendid. Do you need another platter for the pie?"

"Oh…no. The pie isn't a part of the order. It's for Br… Mr. Hollingsworth."

"Very well. I'll place it in his refrigerator. If you need anything, I'll be in the kitchen."

Matilda slid the pie off of the container Tiffani held, and for a moment she thought about not giving it to her. She'd made it especially for Broderick, making sure each ingredient was measured perfectly, and for some reason she didn't want anyone else to touch it.

"Okay. Thank you," she said, trying to muster an upbeat tone.

Tiffani spent the next few minutes arranging the cupcakes on the crystal platters, then she topped each one with a fondant rose. She felt weird being in Broderick's home considering she didn't even know if he was there or not. She'd wanted to ask Matilda but decided against it when she had almost said his first name. She'd noted a twinkle in the housekeeper's eye and Tiffani figured Matilda probably had assumed she had a crush on her handsome, rich employer. Which wasn't far from the truth, but seeming desperate wasn't her personality. Besides, she was there to do a job, not chat with Broderick.

"Hi there."

Tiffani's heart skipped as soon as she heard the sexy, deep voice behind her that belonged to the man she couldn't stop fantasizing about. It washed a load of goose bumps over her body and her eyes closed for a second. She almost put her finger in the last cupcake as she placed it on the platter. Exhaling, she reminded herself Broderick was a customer, not her next boyfriend. Pivoting, she was grateful she was dressed appropriately in a pair of gray dress slacks and a black sweater as opposed to the tank top that had her breasts on display.

"Hi." She held back a wow as her eyes scanned his handsome features. Every time she saw him he was impeccably dressed in a suit and freshly shaven as if he'd literally just left the barber's chair.

He strode over to her and glanced at the cupcakes. "I didn't know you were coming. I would've been down here earlier to greet you."

"It was last minute. My assistant had an emergency."

"Too bad, but at least I get to see you again. You should stay. A lot of investors are going to be here. They're always looking for new businesses to back if you ever decide to expand."

"Thank you for inviting me, but I have to be at my son's karate tournament at 7:30."

He nodded as if he understood, and she appreciated

that. A couple of men she'd gone out with didn't seem to comprehend that her son came first.

"Okay, definitely leave some business cards next to the cupcakes."

"I will. Matilda placed your sweet potato pie in the refrigerator." She grabbed her purse from a chair at the dining room table and pulled a stack of business cards from the inside pocket.

"Thank you. I was wondering if you'd remember. When you emailed the invoice, I didn't see it."

"On the house."

"I appreciate that and the delicious bear claws, but if you keep giving your desserts away you won't make a profit."

"Not true at all. Didn't you take Marketing 101? You give away free products and they keeping coming back for more but as loyal paying customers. You ordered cupcakes after tasting just one at the reception."

Stepping directly into her personal space, a sinful grin emerged across his ruggedly handsome face. "I only ordered them to see you again. I could give a damn about cupcakes, even though yours are delicious. And you're right. I'm definitely coming back for more and *more* just to lay eyes on the breathtaking baker I can't stop thinking about." He traveled a gentle finger down her cheek and paused it on her lips, which parted on demand. "You are too tempting to resist."

Tiffani cursed inwardly at her mouth betraying her. Sucking in her breath, she stepped back, but when she did, all she felt was the wall next to the dessert table. His dark eyes held hers in a deep trance that could only be broken by a magical spell in a fairy-tale world far, far away. He hadn't moved and neither had she. Even when the chef came in the room with a dish that smelled like roast beef and exited as quickly as he'd came in.

Before she could speak, Broderick yanked her body to his. As a surprised gasp escaped her, he pushed them out a side door she hadn't noticed. Tiffani glanced around briefly to see where they were but could only make out a leather couch before he lowered his lips to hers in a subtle, sweet kiss. A part of her wanted to protest, but his mouth on hers caused fervent moaning, which only caused him to sink deeper into her as she willingly responded. Running her hands up his beard, a muffled groan resonated from his throat and he clasped her bottom tight, bringing her body even closer to his hard one. Tiffani loved the sounds they made and the intensity of their connection as he continued twirling his tongue with hers. She'd imagined him kissing her passionately but now, in reality, he was even more powerful and ardent than she'd deemed possible. He was all man. No denying that, especially when he lifted her up like she weighed nothing and carried her to the couch as their lips never left each other's. Sitting down with her straddling his lap, he broke their kiss and stared at her with a heated yet adoring gaze. But before she knew it she had lowered her lips furiously to his once again.

Tiffani knew she needed to stop this charade, but

his tantalizing manly scent was fogging her common sense and all she desired at that moment was more of him. She ran her hands across his chest and down his solid abs until she settled at his belt. She had the urge to yank it off and throw it somewhere in the room. Instead, she grasped it tightly as their kissing manifested more with each passing second. She let out a loud, disappointed gasp as his lips left hers and his tongue explored her neck while clutching her hips and pushing her body even farther on his. She didn't even think that was possible until she felt a slight bulge through his pants, causing electric bolts to shoot through her and end at her center, which was exactly where she wanted him. Broderick had awakened a desire in her that had been suppressed for many years.

Gripping his belt tighter, Tiffani tried to restrain herself from unbuckling it. She couldn't believe her thought process. True, it had been a long time since she'd been intimate with a man, but this wasn't the time or place. Removing her hand from his belt, she wrapped fingers around his neck and he smiled lazily at her.

"Goodness, I wish people weren't on their way over here," he muttered against her ear. "I'll cancel if you tell me to," he said in a gruff tone, tugging at her bottom lip as the doorbell chimed.

"Mmm…as nice as that feels, you are expecting guests."

"Who cares," he whispered, "I'd rather be here with you, beautiful."

She pulled away from him reluctantly as the second chime reminded her she needed to leave.

Gliding her fingers through her hair, she knew it had to be a mess thanks to him running his hands in it. Normally, she hated a single strand being out of place, but right now a disheveled appearance was well worth it. "I believe your guests are arriving, and I really have to get going. If I don't leave now, I'll be late." She glanced at her watch and realized she had less than forty-five minutes to jet across town.

He stood and kissed her lightly on the lips. "I understand. Your son is your first priority. Perhaps we can get together for dinner this weekend?"

"I don't think that's a great idea, Broderick." She stepped back as her senses became unclouded. When he mentioned KJ, she considered that perhaps a date was too much, too soon.

Puzzlement crossed his features. "That was some kiss."

"Yes, yes it was, but I don't want things to move too fast with us. We should get to know each other on more of a friend level first."

"Friend? Mmm…friends don't kiss like that, sweetheart…" He paused as the doorbell rang again and male voices could be heard in the next room.

"I have to run," she said, pulling her keys out of her purse. "Is there another way out to the garage area?" she asked, looking around the wood-paneled room that she now realized was the library.

"Straight through those French doors," he said, pointing toward a row of doors that led outside. "I'll walk you out."

"No need. You should go greet your business associates, and I really need to skedaddle to my car." She began to fast walk but he was on her heels. He opened the door for her and she stepped out but turned around quickly. "You should wipe that hot pink lipstick off before someone sees you." She reached into her purse and pulled out a wet wipe.

Laughing, he took it from her and wiped his lips. "You are definitely a mother. I bet you have hand sanitizer, peppermints, bandages and snacks in there," he teased.

"Yep, along with Neosporin and Children's Tylenol."

"I can believe it. You have my number, so send me a text so I'll know you arrived safely."

"Will do."

Somewhat bewildered, Broderick locked the door back and strode through the main entrance of the library, heading to the foyer. He couldn't believe he'd just told Tiffani to text him when she arrived at her destination. Not that he wasn't a concerned type of person, but normally when a woman left, she left. She was different. This woman had him up at night reading her blog and her social media sites. He wasn't even on social media himself. He didn't see the point in taking selfies, stating what he ate for lunch or what song was "now playing" in the background. None of that held any importance to anyone besides himself. However, reading her cute little catchphrases and seeing what she was up to daily made him crave to know even more. When he had kissed her—which surprised him, as well—he felt like he knew Tiffani. Her wanting to be friends first seemed kind of odd considering he knew everything about her, just from her online presence. *Friend?* The word irked him, but he'd go along with it just to be near her and to respect her wishes. He had a feeling it would be worth it.

Clearing his throat, he straightened his tie and entered the great room. Some of his colleagues were mingling and a few were waiting in line at the bar. He spotted Josh and headed over to him.

"I was looking for you," Josh started. "Matilda mumbled something about a pastry chef and walked out." He raised a blond eyebrow with a smirk. "You weren't getting busy with a pastry chef were you?"

Normally, Broderick would tell the truth when it came to the women he was pursuing or dating, though this time he didn't. There was something about Tiffani he wanted to keep all to himself.

"I have no idea what Matilda is referring to. Is Jeffrey Benson from Benson and Smith Enterprises here? I liked his ideas from the mixer we attended on Saturday, but I need more information before proceeding."

"He's on the list but hasn't yet arrived. However,

Carl Tandy and Cedric Diggs are here, as well as Devin Montgomery from Supreme Construction."

"Cool. I saw him at the wedding I attended and invited him to come this evening. His company is building new lakefront subdivisions in North Carolina, and I'm interested in investing. Make sure you set up a meeting with him."

"No problem, boss. I'll go speak to him now while you see what Carl and Cedric are cooking up in the investment department," Josh stated as the two gentlemen in question approached.

The men shook hands, grabbed some cocktails and retreated to the library to discuss their next business venture in private. Upon entering, Broderick smelled Tiffani's perfume still lingering in the air. His mind drifted back to savoring her delectable lips and the warmth of her skin under his hands. However, he couldn't think about that right now. Even though it was hard not to, considering her scent surrounded him as he now sat in the same spot he had just a few moments ago.

"Josh tells me you two have some new project ideas."

Carl nodded as he sipped his drink. "Yes, along with two other possible investors and hopefully you."

"Tell me about it."

"Well, there's this outdoor shopping area in Dekalb County not too far from the Perimeter Mall area. The property value is high but the stores in the shopping center are old and need some updating. Heck, they may even need to be torn down, but we won't really know until an inspection is done. The man who owns the place is ready to retire and move to Florida and is selling at a reasonable price. We'd love to buy it, tear it down if necessary and rebuild with high-end stores. The places that are already there could stay at a higher lease once their current one runs out. Some are national chains like Starbucks and some are locally owned businesses."

Broderick stirred the ice cubes around in his bourbon. "Mmm…not sure if I want to invest in a strip mall. What else you got?"

"It's not a strip mall," Cedric interjected. "It would be one of those work, live and play areas with condos or lofts, eateries, and so on. There's some vacant property behind it that's for sale, too. About two hundred acres, so we can expand. We've done it before with the other group we used to invest with and you were quite happy with the results."

"Still not sold. I'm looking for something different this go-round. What was the other project?"

"Well…the other one is similar, just a different location. It's in the Stone Mountain area. However, we're also contemplating a famous restaurant chain here in Atlanta. Rumor has it they want to expand to adjoining states."

Broderick nodded as he soaked in the information. He was most interested in the restaurant chain. "I am searching for something new to invest in, but you know I don't just put my name on anything or write a check until I have every detail. Send Josh the information so he can start gathering data to determine the best choice to go with. Anything else?"

Carl shook his head. "Nope, that is all for now. We'll contact Josh if anything else comes up."

"Great." Broderick stood as his cell phone vibrated in his shirt pocket. He withdrew it and saw a text from Tiffani. "If you gentlemen would excuse me I need to take this. Help yourself to the food in the dining room. Chef Crenshaw really outdid himself this time."

He retreated outside on the veranda so he could read her text in private.

Made it to KJ's tournament just in time. Talk to you later. ☺

Broderick smiled at the cute smiley face. It was so like her and her girlie personality. Rejoining his guests, he chatted for the rest of the evening, but he wasn't really focused on discussing any of their money-making opportunities. He kept thinking about Tiffani's scrumptious lips on his and the soft purrs from her mouth. He didn't know how long she expected them to just be friends before he was able to kiss her again. But he also understood her husband had died not too long ago, and she probably wanted to take things slowly. However, it was the sweetest kiss he'd ever tasted and he was hungry for more.

"Thank you for saving me a seat, Preston." Tiffani plopped down between her brother, two years her senior, and their dad on the bleachers at the karate tournament. "Has KJ gone yet?" She bit into her chicken and pecan salad, sighing with relief. She hated the days when she was too busy to eat, and she also hated buying a salad from a fast-food restaurant, but it was that or remain hungry.

"No, his group is next," Preston said, then whispered, "Why do you smell like cologne?"

Darn it. She'd been so busy inhaling the remnants of Broderick's enticing scent embedded on her skin that it never occurred to her that others could smell it, too.

"Huh…what?" Tiffani tried to stare straight ahead. If she looked at her brother, he'd see right through whatever lie she told. She also sensed her father's eyes on her.

"You heard me. You were late. You're never late. Did you have a date?"

"Shh. We're being rude." She took a bite of the salad and chewed slowly so she wouldn't have to speak and hopefully he'd leave her alone. At least for now.

Tiffani continued to stare straight ahead as the kindergarten group did their routine, but she wasn't paying attention. Instead, her thoughts led her back to Broderick's strong, manly embrace and his wicked tongue dancing with hers while his sensual hands cruised over her body. He'd driven her insane with his handling of her and in just a short time, he'd unearthed a passion she didn't know she possessed, and she wanted more. More of him. His intoxicating scent that still lingered, only added more to the erotic feelings she was experiencing. She couldn't believe she'd had the nerve to reach for his tie and belt and had had to restrain herself from doing so. She'd been on a couple of dates since her husband's passing and had a few first kisses but nothing to the point of being blown away. Broderick's kiss made her feel like a desired woman, which was new, exciting and scary.

Tiffani had met Keith their freshman year of college and he'd been her first and only sexual experience. However, she wasn't turned off by the idea of having sex with another man. Far from it, and earlier Broderick confirmed that. She was grateful she'd had to leave and that he had a party to host. If not, things may have gotten more intense, if that were even possible. She may have also done something that in her heart she *wouldn't* have regretted. Being with Broderick was awakening, and she couldn't remember the last time she'd felt so sexual and free.

Have I ever? she pondered. Because of Keith's treatment of her during their marriage, she'd fallen out of love with him and sex became a chore that she hated but only did because she felt obligated.

Even though she never wanted to remarry, the option of a male companion was fine as long as it was understood that their relationship would never lead to marriage or living together. She enjoyed her independence and control over her life and couldn't fathom another man tearing her down with his words and ridicule.

When she'd told Broderick she wanted to get to know him better on a friend level before proceeding further, she meant it. A man with his power and money could be a controlling jerk like her husband had been. She had to make sure he wasn't before venturing into another relationship. She'd witnessed male chauvinistic signs with Keith while they were in college but they'd been subtle and didn't become full-blown until a year into their marriage. She had been contemplating divorce when he'd had a heart attack while driving home from work and died on the way to the hospital.

Tiffani had felt awful about it for awhile. She'd never wished death on him because their son had been four at the time and worshiped the ground he walked on. If she'd gone through with the divorce, she would've made sure Keith saw his son whenever he wanted.

"He's up next," her father, John Chase, stated.

Tiffani clapped and grabbed her cell phone out of her purse to record her son's part in the tournament. Even though KJ didn't have a father, he had plenty of father figures. Her father, brother and her cousin Braxton Chase were all very present in her son's life. They took him to get his hair cut, attended Atlanta Hawks and Atlanta Falcon games, played sports at the park and enjoyed other boy activities that a father normally would do with his son. She was grateful. Even though his dad was dead, KJ never missed a beat and was a fun-loving, intelligent and well-rounded eight-year-old boy. Tiffani sometimes feared he would eventually begin acting like

Keith as far as the male chauvinist side, but so far he hadn't. Considering his three father figures weren't, she hoped he would take after them.

"There's my handsome grandson!"

"Let's go, nephew!" Preston clapped loudly.

"That's my baby!" Tiffani cheered and then pressed play on the video app on her cell phone.

An hour later, Tiffani ran out to the gym floor to meet KJ halfway as he sprinted toward her with his second-place trophy. She picked him up and twirled him around.

"I'm so proud of you! We'll add this to the collection," she said, putting him down. He may always be her baby, but he was no longer small and was too heavy to hold for too long.

"Thanks, Mommy. You think Daddy was watching?"

"Of course," she answered sincerely. "He's your guardian angel and will always watch over you."

"And he watches over you, too," he stated matter-of-factly.

"Yes, me, too." *I hope not after that steamy kiss today.* "Let's show Grandpa and Uncle Preston and then we're off to a celebratory dinner at wherever you want to go!"

"Now that sounds like a plan," KJ said, pulling her by the hand toward her father and brother as they walked out to the floor.

While KJ showed his grandfather some of his karate moves, Preston pulled Tiffani to the side, and she prayed he wasn't back on the topic he had started before the tournament. Ever since she'd told her brother what really had gone on in her marriage, Preston had been furious that she hadn't confided in him before Keith had died. However, she knew if she would've, he and the rest of the Chase men would've pummeled Keith. So, instead she acted as if everything was peachy and had only told Megan bits and pieces when she needed to confide in someone.

"I noticed some of the mothers checking you out," she started before he could even open his mouth.

"Well, you know they can't help but notice all this fineness," he teased.

She reached up and ruffled his curly, silky hair. "Geez, you're so modest. How's Kay?"

He shrugged nonchalantly. "I don't know. Not seeing her anymore. Talking to this other chick I met at Phipps Plaza last week."

"You think it may get serious?" Tiffani wasn't one of those sisters to nag her big brother about settling down, but he had always talked about having a wife and family one day. However, he wasn't dating women he would consider marrying.

"Nah…she's cool, though. And I haven't forgotten our conversation, sis." Preston's expression and tone turned serious.

"What are you talking about?" she asked as if she had no clue.

"The cologne you're wearing."

"I'm not wearing cologne. It's from a perfume sample I was given at the mall and it's just strong. I'm definitely not going to buy it. You know I prefer light sweet fragrances, and this one is just entirely too much for my pheromones. It only smells good in the bottle."

Tiffani hated lying to Preston, but she knew how overprotective he was when it came to her dating life. Plus, she wasn't ready to discuss Broderick with him or anyone else for that matter.

Preston raised an eyebrow followed by a snicker at her long, drawn-out answer.

"Okay, you don't have to talk about it. I just want you happy," he said sincerely, kissing her forehead.

She interlocked her arm with his and stared up at her brother as they strolled behind KJ and their father. "Trust me, I am."

Chapter 4

Broderick tried to read over Supreme Construction's financial information in the back of his Bentley, but he couldn't concentrate on business. He was on his way to have lunch with Tiffani. They'd been having a friendly courtship for over a week, chatting on the phone and him stopping by to see her using the excuse of buying Danishes or a slice of cheesecake. No more sweet kisses, but he'd noticed a glimmer in her eyes whenever he entered the shop. They'd mostly discuss their daily lives and long-term plans. She loved talking about her son and all of his accomplishments in school as well as his karate tournaments. She hadn't mentioned much about her marriage. He had decided not to pry, fearing the subject may upset her. He assumed a part of her missed her late husband and still grieved.

After grabbing a few sandwiches and salads from a deli in the same shopping plaza, he entered the bakery, which was half full of customers. He spotted Kendall at the cash register but didn't see Tiffani. He figured she was in her office.

"Hey, Kendall. Where's your boss?" he asked in an upbeat tone.

She shook her head as a grim expression formed on her face. Once a lady she was assisting left, Kendall leaned over the counter and whispered, "You really don't want to see her right now."

"Why not?" he asked. Tiffani was always in a great mood.

"Um…she's mad… No…angry."

He wrinkled his brow. "Where is she?"

"In her office. Enter at your own risk."

He walked through the kitchen where Tiffani's other employee and assistant baker, Mindy, was making cheesecakes and knocked lightly on the office door. He didn't know what could be wrong. He'd spoken to her that morning before she'd headed into a meeting and she'd been her usual chipper self.

"I don't want to be disturbed," she sobbed out.

"It's Broderick with lunch." He tried the door handle, but it was locked. "Let me in, Tiff."

The lock clicked and the door opened. He was astonished to see tears—and mascara—streaming down her face. Something tugged at his heart as he closed the door, and he immediately drew her to him.

"What's wrong, beautiful?"

Her face crumpled as more tears flowed. "Everything," she croaked out. "Everything I've worked hard for…is gone. Just gone." She beat her hands on his chest before backing up and pacing around the small room. "It's not fair. I've worked so hard to get here. Saving every damn penny and clipping coupons. I've sacrificed so much and now there's a strong possibility I could lose it all."

Taking a few long strides toward her, he turned her around to look at him. "What happened?"

Sniffing, she ran her hands through her hair as a frustrated exhale escaped her lips.

"You remember the meeting I had to go to this morning? It was with Harvey Stewart, owner of the plaza, and all of the store owners. He wants to sell Premium Village because his wife is retiring soon and they're moving to Hawaii or something like that. I'm happy for them, but he informed us there are about six different bids on the table for this property. Some of the companies want to tear the place down and start over or remodel, while some plan to leave well enough alone. He said it won't happen until after all of our leases are up in regard to the possibility of this space being torn down. What if I have to start over, find a new place for my business? Even though there may be an option of coming back here, I'm sure the lease would be higher and I can barely afford the one I have now."

Tiffani began sobbing again, and he wrapped his

arms tightly around her, rocking her back and forth. Stroking her hair, he kissed her forehead and whispered, "I'm here. Let it all out, beautiful."

Digging her hands into his upper biceps, she buried her head into his chest to muffle her crying. Her shoulders heaved up and down while she stuttered out "it's not fair" over and over. Broderick hated seeing her cry. He hated that she was hurting and wished there was something he could do.

She lifted her head and looked up at him and then down to his suit jacket. "I'm so…sorry. I've got tears and mascara all over your expensive coat."

"Don't worry about that, precious." He kissed her forehead tenderly. "When is this all supposed to take place?"

After wiping her tears followed by a series of sniffing, she looked back up at him. "I don't know. I guess within the next six months or so. His wife is a teacher so she's retiring this upcoming May. I would assume he'd want everything over and done with before that time."

"Things like this happen all the time. It's kind of what I do, but this is a really nice plaza in a great location. I doubt whoever buys it will tear it down anytime soon. I mean, it could use some new signage and other cosmetic improvements but tearing it down would be drastic. It doesn't appear to be older than ten years. Tearing it down wouldn't be feasible for any party involved unless businesses weren't flourishing and it was time for a change. Every time I come over here the parking lot is packed."

"But what if…"

"Stop with your what ifs and think positive. These things take a long time to happen. Appraisals, assessments, inspectors, money and a whole bunch of other stuff. During the interim, start looking for other spots, if that will make you feel better. It's always great to have the next plan or idea in place just in case the first one doesn't work out."

"I searched for other places, but this one was the most conducive because KJ's school is less than ten minutes away. Plus, mine and my parents' homes are around the corner. The other locations I considered are a little farther out. Even though they were slightly cheaper, I needed to be closer to home."

Pulling away from him, she sat in her desk chair and rested her head on the back of it. Closing her eyes, she exhaled as silent tears poured down her stained cheeks. Sliding his silk handkerchief out of his coat pocket, he retreated to the adjoining bathroom and ran the material under the cool water. Upon his return, she was still in the same position but the tears had slowed some. He kneeled in front of her and grabbed her hand.

"Hey, beautiful." He wiped the tears and the mascara off of her face.

She sniffed and smiled weakly. "Thank you, but you're ruining your handkerchief. It matches your tie." Running her hand along his tie, she sniffed and blew her nose in the handkerchief. "You know there are paper towels in the bathroom."

"I know, but I figured they'd be too scratchy for your delicate face and the silk would be better against your soft skin."

"You're so sweet and thoughtful, no matter what anyone else has ever said." She winked and stood, and he did the same. "I'll be okay. You're right. I need to think positive, but I also need to plan just in case."

"Yes, that's a good decision. Hungry?" He clutched her hand and led her to the little bistro table in the corner of her office. She sat down and he grabbed the deli bag from her desk. After they ate in silence for a moment, the businessman in him couldn't help but want to know more.

"Who invested in the bakery with you?"

"No one. I used some of the insurance money from my husband's death, tutored on Saturdays at the Monroe Community Center and basically pinched pennies."

"No bank loan? No family members contributed?"

"Nope. Megan, my dad and my brother offered, but I didn't want to owe anyone anything or have an investor in control of my business. It's just me, myself and I… and KJ of course. He gave me fifty dollars for the paint." She giggled and popped a pickle slice in her mouth.

"Where did he get that kind of money?" When he was KJ's age he barely had fifty cents.

"Birthday money, allowance, chores, etcetera. He saves it in a safe in his closet. Something his dad started doing with him when he was three. Keith was a CPA and had begun teaching KJ how to count and save money. Of course, I didn't really use his money, but he thinks I did, so he says he owns one percent of Sweet Treats."

Broderick smiled. At eight years old the only thing on his mind had been keeping his mother from doing drugs. "I like the way this kid thinks. I'll have to sit down with him and give him some more advice."

"Oh…yeah…one day…" She shrugged and casted her eyes down to her half-eaten turkey sandwich.

He balled up his empty sandwich wrapper and tossed it in a nearby trash can. "Did I say something wrong?"

"Um…no. I just… I mean I don't know if I'm comfortable yet with you meeting KJ."

"We're friends. Remember?" He still couldn't believe he'd let her put him in the friend category.

"Yes, but he'll think differently. He's always asking me if I'm ever going to replace his father. I'm not the type to bring different men around for him to meet and then when it goes nowhere, he has a bunch of uncles who aren't blood-related, you know."

Broderick chewed his food as his thoughts floated to his mom and her so-called boyfriends. Most of them were drug dealers who were in and out of their small one-bedroom apartment in a rough neighborhood on the outskirts of downtown Atlanta. He would be in the bedroom while his mother and her male companion would be getting high in the living room. Sometimes there was laughter and other times he heard his mother's tears. When he'd go to comfort her, she would be in a corner crying, sometimes even wearing bruises.

He understood Tiffani's stance. He'd wished his mother had thought the same, but his environment and experiences had only made him tougher and stronger. He trusted and loved no one. He'd had girlfriends but had never given his heart to anyone. However, something about Tiffani struck a chord in him and for once in a long while his heart beat again.

"I understand, Tiff. Whenever you're ready."

"I'm glad you understand and thank you for lunch and for comforting me. I sincerely appreciate it."

"You're welcome. Is your break almost over?"

"Yep. I gotta go make a last-minute batch of bat- and spider-shaped cookies for KJ's Halloween sleepover tonight."

"House full of kids. Sounds like fun," he said sarcastically, rising to his feet, grabbing his suit jacket from the back of the chair and swinging it over his shoulder. Time always flew when he was with Tiffani.

"Nope. House full of silence. KJ is going to his best friend's house. I'm chilling on the couch with a glass of merlot, pizza and the remote control."

"You know I'm having my annual Halloween party for my employees and some business partners at my home. You should come. You've had a long, stressful day."

"Nah… I just want to unwind and relax. I don't get much alone time once I'm home."

"Well if you change your mind, let me know. I have a meeting, but I'll call you later to check on you." He leaned down and kissed her cheek. "And don't stress, beautiful. It'll work out."

"Thank you. Have fun tonight. Are you dressing up?"

He wrinkled his forehead. *Was she serious?* "Um… hadn't planned on it."

She smacked her lips and swished her lips to the side. "How are you hosting a Halloween party and not dressing up in a costume?"

"I'll go as a businessman."

"There's no fun in that."

He laughed and was glad she was smiling again. "I'll pick up a mask or something on the way home."

"Take pictures and text them to me."

"Right." Twisting the doorknob, he looked back over his shoulder. "Talk to you soon. And everything will work out. I promise."

As he rode to his next meeting, Broderick couldn't help but think about what had happened with Tiffani. Besides his mother, he'd never comforted another woman like that before. He'd seen women cry, usually when he was breaking up with them. But it had never made him feel so awful, even when they'd yell out he was a coldhearted bastard and the most unloving man they'd ever met. He'd shrugged and carried on with his life, but Tiffani crying in his arms pulled on his insides. He was sad for her and it stirred his emotions. That wasn't normal and it scared him. However, he felt a strong connection with her. Strong enough to confide in her about parts of his life he had never wanted to share before, but he sensed Tiffani would understand.

Tiffani sipped her wine and sat at the kitchen island running her fingers along the bouquet of pink and purple peonies that had arrived to the bakery as she was leaving with a card that simply read, "Smile, beautiful." It was signed BJH. She indeed did smile. In fact, she couldn't stop. It was totally unexpected, and after the long day she'd endured, Tiffani appreciated the thoughtful gesture. He'd been full of surprises that day. An hour before the peonies arrived, he'd sent a picture text to her cell phone of a simple black mask and a caption that read: "I'm going as a mysterious businessman." And it wasn't far from the truth. He had remained a mystery to her. He hadn't discussed anything about his personal life other than his day-to-day business. She knew nothing of his family, where he was from or his childhood. He seemed guarded at times but not stand-offish as Megan had stated. However, Broderick was definitely a private person.

Lifting the vase in one hand, she slid her wineglass off the island with the other and headed to the media room to catch up on some television shows saved on her DVR. She set the flowers on the coffee table, settled on the couch and released a long sigh. Pulling her cell phone out of her pajama shirt pocket, she decided to call Broderick before his party began. The phone had barely rung before he answered it.

"Hey, gorgeous. Changed your mind?"

Goodness, his voice sounded like heaven in her ear. She hated to admit it to herself, but she wanted to see him.

"No. I called to say thank you for the lovely peonies. They definitely brightened up my day."

"You're welcome. I had hoped they would. Is KJ at his sleepover?"

"Yep, I'm relaxing with my wine and remote. Has the party started?"

"The first few guests have arrived. I'm in my study watching them on the security monitor. People are actually dressed in costumes. I can't tell who some of them are except the fellas from the mailroom. They're dressed like basketball players. A few others are dressed like vampires and zombies. They have on makeup and shredded clothes like extras from Michael Jackson's Thriller video."

She laughed. "Cool. Take pictures and send them to me."

"Or you can come."

"I would love to, but I've had a glass of wine. I don't drink and drive."

"I'll send my driver."

"No. Besides, I don't have anything to wear." Her

mind drifted upstairs to her closet as she tried to jog her memory of what she could wear...unless she went dressed as a baker. But where was the fun in that?

"You need some excitement. Plus, I bought you a pink mask just in case."

"No you didn't." As soon as she said that, her cell phone chimed, and she switched over to her text messages to see a pink sparkly mask similar to his black one.

"You were saying, Ms. Lake?"

She couldn't help but laugh loudly. "Okay. I'll come."

"Is an hour enough time for you to get dressed?"

"Yes, that's fine."

"Perfect. I can't wait to see you." His tone was casual, but a shiver ran over her. She didn't know why she was so nervous all of sudden. They were becoming good friends, and she enjoyed his company. However, at the same time she knew she could easily fall for him more than she already had. Their heated kiss and being in his warm embrace had pretty much solidified that. She'd never felt so comfortable and content in a man's arms as she had with Broderick earlier that day or the time before. He seemed genuinely concerned and didn't say anything that would hurt her worse or tear her down as Keith would've surely done. He would've found some way to make it seem like it was her fault that the ownership was being taken over by someone else. Then, he would've called her every dumb name possible, unlike the sweet ones Broderick had bestowed upon her.

Beautiful. Precious. Sweetheart. The few times Keith even formed his lips to say those words was when he was Dr. Jekyll, begging for forgiveness, then he'd go back to being Mr. Hyde the next day.

As she rummaged through her closet, Tiffani thought about how thankful she was that that part of her life was over. But in order for her to have peace of mind, she couldn't be in another serious relationship that would lead to marriage. The tight grasp that Keith had had on her nearly ruined her as a person. She had started to become out of touch with who she was as a woman. That couldn't happen again. Even though she really liked Broderick, she felt it was time to let him know what she did and didn't want. She needed to avoid him becoming invested in a relationship that wasn't leading to a long-term commitment, at all costs.

Chapter 5

Broderick chatted with his secretary's husband while his eyes diverted to the door every time Matilda opened it. As instructed, his driver had sent a quick text when he'd arrived at Tiffani's home. Broderick couldn't believe he was antsy over a woman, but he wanted to see her and was curious to see the costume she'd put together at the last minute.

"I appreciate you giving Leslie the week off during spring break so we can take the kids to Disney World. I know it was a spur of the moment trip…"

Broderick tuned back into the conversation. "Nonsense. You won a contest, and that's great. Besides, Leslie could probably use a vacation away from me."

The chime of the doorbell interrupted his conversation once more as Leslie approached to say something, but he didn't hear her. Instead, his vision was focused on the woman in the pink sparkly mask who sashayed in wearing a clingy red pencil skirt and a black off-the shoulder blouse. A short curly wig adorned with a red rose pinned behind her ear, huge gold hoop earrings and a pair of black stilettos completed her outfit. Raking his eyes over her, a strain against his pants emerged when he noted how the mask emphasized her luscious, red lips and the sexy skirt pronounced the curves of her hips. He had to restrain himself from reaching out and grasping them.

Broderick turned to Leslie and her husband, who were still chatting about their upcoming vacation.

"If you two would excuse me, I need to say hello to one of my guests who has just arrived."

He dashed straight to the beauty he'd been waiting for. Taking her hand, he brought it to his lips and kissed it softly.

"Hello, Ms. Jones. So glad you could make it."

A sly smile cross her delicious lips. "Thank you, but please quit with the formalities. Just call me Carmen," she said in a seductive voice.

"The sexy siren herself," he wrapped his arm around her waist and led her through the crowd in the foyer.

"I'm impressed you know who I am."

"Of course. Dorothy Dandridge was one bad lady, and I must say you're definitely doing her justice tonight."

"Thank you," she said, scanning the room. "There are a lot of people here."

He nodded as they trekked over to the bar that was draped in black tulle decorated with silver cats and orange pumpkins. "About two hundred and I expect a few more."

"All these people work for you?"

"Not all. Some of them brought their spouses or significant others and some are business partners or golf buddies. I invited Bryce and Sydney, but they weren't able to make it."

"Yeah, they're at the Monroe Community Center. I baked a lot of goodies for that event. Instead of trick or treating, it's a safe-night lock-in with games and kiddie movies."

"Great idea. Let's grab a drink, some food and retreat some place in private where we can chat."

She studied him with puzzlement. "Aren't you hosting a party?"

"My guests will be fine."

After filling their plates, they moved to his private quarters upstairs and into his home office. She placed her food on the coffee table in the sitting area by the fireplace but she didn't sit. Instead she strode to the mantel, picked up the picture and studied it before placing it back.

"That's my mother," he said, settling on the couch.

"You two have the same smile and eyes. She's beautiful."

"Yes, she was," he said quietly.

"Was? I'm so sorry to hear that." She was silent for a moment as she eyed him carefully. "How long ago did she pass?"

"I was eight years old."

"Oh…you were KJ's age." She sat on the chaise longue in front of the fireplace and curled her feet under her. "Do you have any siblings?" She reached over and grabbed a mini quiche from her plate.

"I'm sure my father has some more children somewhere."

"Did he raise you after your mother died?"

"Nah…he's been in and out of my life. In a way, I raised myself."

"No grandparents? Aunts?"

"I lived with my maternal grandmother but she was ill and died soon after. My aunt took me in but she had six children and issues of her own. I was a burden, as she told me over and over. I stayed with different family members who felt the same way and even in a few foster homes after I ran away from another aunt who refused to let me return when the police found me. Things turned around when my guidance counselor in high school persuaded me to take the college entrance exams. My grades were decent. They would've been better if I hadn't moved around so much. Luckily I was in a group home owned by a Lutheran church my senior year so I had some stability and security. I went to the University of Tennessee in Chattanooga and majored in business. After I received my MBA, I started working for a consulting firm here in Atlanta. I got my big break when I invested fifty thousand of my retirement savings into a restaurant franchise, and after a few more investments, here I am. That's my rags to riches story."

She smiled like a proud mother. "Well, you definitely have a success story. Are you close with your family now that you're an adult?"

He chuckled sarcastically. "I'm somewhat estranged from them. Growing up they told me I'd amount to nothing. That all my silly dreams of becoming a millionaire were unrealistic and that I'd never make it out of the hood except behind bars or in a casket."

"Oh, Broderick. I'm so sorry."

"Don't be, beautiful. Their negativity made me more determined to succeed and prove them all wrong. My mother wasn't like that, though. She was encouraging and loving. She never doubted for a second that I would accomplish my goals even when I was just a kid. She used to say, 'Son, fly with the eagles and not the turkeys.' That's been my motto my entire life. I just wish she was here to experience all of this with me. I'd spoil her rotten," he said, laughing and wiping a few tears away.

Rising, Tiffani leaned over and kissed his cheek. "I'm sure you would and I bet she's in heaven smiling down on you."

"I know she is. I can always feel her love. She's the only person in this world who has ever truly loved me."

Tiffani's expression turned solemn as she frowned with sad eyes. "Really? No girlfriend or best friend...?"

"I've had girlfriends if you want to call them that, but I've never been in love with any of them. Don't think I'm even capable of doing so. My mom has been the only person I've ever loved."

"Oh." She sat back on the chaise and was silent for a moment. "Do you know where your father is?"

"Oh yeah. He's in a retirement community about an hour outside of Atlanta. I pay for it." He shrugged, strolled over to the wet bar and poured a scotch.

"Are you cool with your dad?"

"No. He's in the same category with the rest of them. I tried to have a relationship with him when I moved back to Atlanta, but he just kept telling me I'd fail. He's the reason I pretty much emptied my 401k and made my first investment. I wanted to prove him wrong."

"Do you visit him?"

He leaned on the edge of his desk and crossed his feet. "No, not really. We talk on the phone every once and awhile when he needs or wants something. His doctor sends me updates on his health."

"Well, the holidays are coming up. Maybe you should go see him."

"I don't know." He stirred the ice around in his glass. "Perhaps."

The grandfather clock in the corner chimed nine times, interrupting their conversation, for which he was grateful.

"Oh my. Your guests are probably wondering where you are." Standing, she grabbed her mask from the mantel and placed it over her eyes. "Why are you just sitting there casually drinking your scotch? You have a party going on downstairs."

"Trust me. There's plenty of food and booze. They're not looking for me, and if they are, it's probably to discuss a business idea. I'm not interested in that at the moment."

"But aren't some of your friends here? I'm sure they're wondering where you're hiding."

"I don't have family and friends surrounding me all the time. My life is pretty much business. Most of my *friends*, as you say, are colleagues. Sure, we play golf, meet for drinks and attend parties, but it's all business."

She slipped the mask off and placed a hand on her hip. "Oh, I see. So hanging with me is all business?" she asked in a firm tone.

"Honestly, I don't know why I'm hanging out with you, but I've enjoyed every moment of it. When I'm with you, I never even think about business. My mind turns clouded, and I get lost in your sweet smile."

Her stern expression softened a tad and then she spoke softly. "You know my life hasn't always been perfect." She strolled over to where he was and sat in one of the Queen Anne-style chairs in front of his desk.

"Do tell." He sipped his drink and wondered what her story entailed.

"I was married to the devil."

* * *

Tiffani surprised herself with the words she'd spoken out loud. Maybe it was the wine or the fact that Broderick had opened up to her. She hated talking or thinking about her life with Keith because that book in her past was closed and sealed shut.

"Wow, I wasn't expecting you to say that. Wait… you didn't kill him, did you?" he teased, hoisting himself up on his desk. "You beautiful ones are always the crazy ones."

"Ha-ha. No, I didn't kill him. He had a heart attack while driving home from work. He slammed into the side rail on the interstate and died on the way to the hospital."

"Was he abusive?"

"Yes. Verbally and mentally. Never physically. But he hadn't always been like that. We'd dated off and on in college and married after graduation. Everything was fine until a year into our marriage when I told him I wanted to go back to school to get my master's degree with some of my teacher friends at work. I had planned on eventually receiving my specialist degree or even a doctorate degree. Both my parents were principals at elementary schools at the time and that was also a goal of mine. Anyway, I'd already started filling out the application, but he snapped when I told him. He said I was following behind my friends, which wasn't the case at all. Keith knew in college that I wanted to obtain advanced degrees. I reminded him that with each degree,

I'd make more money. He went on and on about how he takes care of me and what I made was enough. Also, he was adamant that when we started a family, I wouldn't have time for school."

"Oh, he was one of those brothers. Didn't want you to make too much because then you'd be financially independent."

"Yep, he was the epitome of a male chauvinist. I kind of knew that in college but I guess I thought he would change, not get worse."

"So did you get your masters?"

"No. I ended up pregnant a few months later and he wanted me to stay home with KJ and have about three more children. That's not what we'd discussed in pre-marriage counseling. I was only going to take off a year, but he said that he didn't want strangers taking care of his child at day care."

"You didn't remind him about the agreement?"

"Yep and he called me a trifling, ungrateful bitch. That was his pet name for me because that's all he called me along with other degrading words."

"Beautiful, I'm so sorry you went through that. Don't you have a brother because if you were my sister…"

"I didn't tell Preston or anyone, except for Megan, until after Keith died. She and I are very close so she knew mostly everything. While I hate that he died because of our son, I'm glad that part of my life is over. I used to be a fun, happy person. I did a lot of pretending around my family and friends while married to Keith.

I'd make up excuses that I couldn't make it places because KJ had a fever or an ear infection. If I went out with my cousins or friends for lunch, I'd lie and say I needed to pick KJ up from his grandparents or the babysitter by a certain time. But this was all because Keith wanted me home before he got home from work. And the few times I was late he'd curse me out and by late I mean on the dot. After awhile, I just stopped spending time with my family and friends just to keep the peace in my own home and, of course, for KJ's sake."

"Why didn't you divorce him?"

"That was the plan. I'd confided in Megan because the creep somehow could see all my text messages."

"How do you know that?"

"Once, I'd texted Megan something about her ex-boyfriend who was a total jerk because he'd cheated on her, and Keith said tell Megan she should give the doctor another chance when he had gotten home from work that day. I was confused because I hadn't told him about it. I asked him how he knew and he casually responded 'I saw your conversation. I've had access to your messages for almost two years' and then he strode out of the room as if that were an okay thing to do. I confronted him about it and he told me he paid every single bill and I was his effing wife and he had a right to know what I discussed."

"He was psycho. I'm so sorry, precious."

"Yes, he was. I was never big on texting so he didn't see much of anything but the thought of him violating my privacy was just pathetic. The next day we had a family function at my cousin Braxton's jazz club, and I pulled Megan in the bathroom and told her about the text messages and wanting to divorce Keith. I gave her roughly five hundred dollars that I'd saved from leftover change and some birthday money my dad had given me. My husband watched what I spent like a hawk, so she opened an account in her name so I'd have money to file for the divorce."

"I thought most women had their own mad money checking account. I hear my secretary talking about buying clothes and hiding them from her husband, even though I don't think he cares."

"Yeah, I had one when we first got married, but he said some crap about being one and that meant our accounts, as well. I actually fell for that mess."

Broderick washed his hands over his face. "I'm sorry the bastard's dead because of KJ, but I'm glad you're not in hell anymore. I'm sure your next husband won't be like that."

Tiffani shook her head vigorously. "There won't be a next husband. I'm *never* getting married again."

"I don't blame you one bit, but what about a steady boyfriend?" He rested his hand on his chin.

"Um… I'm kind of open to that or a companion that I can hang out with and go to dinner and events. Perhaps travel, but I wouldn't call him my boyfriend. That's so high school. I'd just want to be."

"Be what?" he asked as his forehead indented.

She laughed. It was the first time she'd spoken her idea out loud. "I know it sounds weird. But I want to just *be* in the moment, not in a relationship where I can't make my own decisions and feel as though I'm suffocating. I refuse to be treated the way Keith treated me ever again. Broderick, there were times when I looked in the mirror and I didn't know who was staring back. I lost my confidence, my voice and my strength during those six years. I lost me. I can't let another man control and degrade me. I have my son to consider, my peace of mind and my sanity."

"So this be-in-the-moment relationship? Would it be with more than one dude?"

"Oh no. Definitely no."

"Would this be an intimate relationship, as well?"

She noted the arrogant rise of his curious smile. "Yes, I would hope so and he'd have to be really great in bed."

"I see." He sipped his scotch and studied her with dark, amorous eyes. "Anything else?"

"He'd have to be someone I can confide in and trust. Not someone who would want to know my finances or try to control my life. At the end of the day, I make my own decisions."

"Go 'head, Janet, or Ms. Jackson if you're nasty," he joked. "You call your own shots, beautiful."

She giggled. "You're hilarious. I love when you call me beautiful."

"That's because you are. Inside and out."

Truth, seduction and lust were all laced into his

words and his stare. She bit her bottom lip and ran her hand slowly along her bare neck, down to her collarbone and across the top of her cleavage as a slight mist of sweat formed on her skin. Her pulse sped up as he licked his bottom lip LL Cool J style, and she realized what she had just done. She silently hoped Broderick would replace her hand with his tongue.

He slid off the desk and snatched her out of the chair by her waist. His lips hesitated over hers as he stared into her eyes and beyond. Tiffani could taste the scent of his scotch and wanted to savor more. Her body quivered in his commanding embrace as raw pleasure journeyed throughout her veins.

When he lowered his lips an extra half inch to hers, it felt like their first kiss all over again. Broderick explored her appealing mouth slowly. He wanted to become familiar with every crevice of it just in case a while passed before she let him near her again. However, the thought of that caused an intense churn in his stomach, and he delved deeper so she would always crave for him to kiss and caress her. She was radiant, and the moans erupting from her mouth were driving him insane. Pivoting them, he placed her on the desk and gazed at her as he slowly pulled the hem of her skirt up her legs until it reached mid-thigh. Not once did she flinch, blink or protest. Instead, a sinful smile emerged, and she wrapped her long legs around his waist.

"Take off your coat," she whispered against his lips.

Wasting no time, he followed her demand and flung it to the floor.

Nibbling her bottom lip, he slid a hand on her lacy panties. "Now you have to take off something." He continued rubbing her in a circular fashion as her breathing became slightly unhinged, but she still didn't appear unruffled. Instead, she was quite composed, and he was determined to change that soon.

"What do you want me to take off?" Running her hands up his face she kissed him slow and deep, turning her tongue hard around his.

"Everything," he growled in her mouth.

"Just one item. I'll even let you pick."

Slipping his finger around the waistband of her panties, he tugged on them as she lifted her bottom. He glided them down as she detached her legs from around him and bent them so he could remove the black lacy thong around her heels.

"How about that wig, too."

"Fair enough." She reached up and unpinned it from her hair, which was wrapped around her head. She took out a couple more hair pins and combed her fingers though her tresses until they fell wild and straight around her.

"Better?"

"Absolutely," he answered in a raspy tone while rustling his fingers through her silky threads.

Wrapping her legs tightly around him again, she

yanked him by the shirt and lowered backward to the desk with him following on top of her.

"I think you're taking this control thing a little too far, don't you?" he teased.

"Shut up and kiss me."

Before he could, she reached her lips up and he sunk his tongue into her mouth with more zest with every passing second. He hated to leave her delectable lips, but there were other parts of her body where his tongue yearned to feast as it traveled down her neck. Her hands dug into his shoulders and her head thrashed. The sounds rushing from her were exactly the ones he wanted to hear. He wanted to fluster her and drive her crazy, just as she'd done to him the second he'd laid eyes on her. While his mouth concentrated on ravishing her neck, one of his hands glided back between her legs. There was no lacy material in the way this time. Just warm, moist skin. He massaged the area with his hand in an unhurried, circular motion, increasing the pressure each time her legs shuddered around him. Lifting his lips from her neck, he placed them on her lips but he didn't kiss her. Instead, he watched her pant heavily and her hands tightly clutch the desk as her back arched up and then down.

"Oh, Broderick. Oh…mmm…um… I…" she huffed incoherently. "Brod…"

"What, baby? Is this what you want?" he asked, sinking his hand farther until one finger teased along the opening.

She moaned loudly, removed one of her legs from around him and set her heeled foot on his desk. "Yessssss...right there."

Sliding the finger in, he shook at the tightness and slickness of her. He could only imagine how something else would feel nestled warmly inside of her. Just the mere thought caused it to strain and push against his pants.

"That's perfect," she mumbled. "Don't stop."

And he didn't as he continued sliding it in and out while he kept his eyes focused on her passionate facial expressions and the erotic sounds she made. She squirmed and jerked on the desk and even reached down to hold his hand as the rush of an orgasm caused her to shudder frantically. She held on to his shoulders tightly and stomped her heels on his desk. Normally he was somewhat of an ass when it came to the protection of his belongings, but he really didn't care at the moment that there were more than likely scratches on the mahogany. Broderick only wanted to satisfy the woman he couldn't stop thinking about. The woman he couldn't get enough of. She was under him with her wild hair spread across the desk and sweat dripping from her body. She was yelling obscenities and words he couldn't quite make out but he didn't care because she was breathtakingly beautiful inside and out. He only wanted to bring her pleasure however she needed it.

Once she simmered down, he lifted her back up and kissed her damp forehead.

"What else would you like me to do?"

* * *

Tiffani froze at his words. There was more he wanted to do? She was still coming down from the high he'd sent her on and he actually wanted to do more? The strong orgasm she'd experienced was still coursing throughout her veins like a shuttle taking off to the moon. She was completely satisfied. Wiping her damp brow, she smiled lazily at him.

"I'm good and to be honest I'm not ready to have sex with you yet."

"That's not a problem, beautiful. When we finally go the distance, I don't want a bunch of guests in my home. I can't be restricted to just the bedroom."

"Oh…well, what else did you have in mind?" Her body trembled with anticipation of what else he could do. She was already floating above the clouds. "I'm not removing any more articles of clothing."

Sporting a mischievous grin, he laid her back on the desk. Raising an eyebrow, she swished her lips to the side and wondered what the heck he was going to do next.

"You don't have to. It's already removed and in here." He patted his shirt pocket that held her panties. "And what else do I have in mind?" Leaning over her, he kissed her gently, which released a sigh from her. "I want to taste you and by you, I don't mean your mouth." He kissed her, swirling his tongue like an erratic driver.

She broke away from his lips. "Wait? You mean?"

"Yes." Lingering his lips over hers, he roamed his

hand down her body and back to her center. He slid his tongue over to her ear. "My mouth is literally watering for you. Can I have a taste, sweetheart?"

"Um…sure." Tiffani tried not to stutter her words and held back a gulp, but she couldn't admit to him that at thirty-two years old, no one had ever done what he was about to do. The only man she'd been with was Keith, and he had refused to do it.

For a moment, she felt like a virgin all over again waiting in fear and eagerness as Broderick started at the indent in her neck and licked down until he reached a few inches below her belly button. Her body trembled uncontrollably as she waited. The moment she closed her eyes, she felt the tip of his tongue and her eyes shot wide open, then shut again at the magnitude of his first subtle lick.

He continued licking and nibbling on her in circles, back and forth and some other crazy way. She really didn't care how he kissed her there. It all felt insanely wonderful.

How had her poor body been deprived of this all this time? Her twin cousins had always discussed how much they'd enjoyed it. She'd just wrinkle her nose and wouldn't disclose her sex life with Keith. The truth was she just didn't know it could be this damn good.

"Goodness, you're amazing." She didn't know how the words even came out as she was breathless and parched. A loud gasp exploded from her mouth as he parted her legs wider and delved his tongue inside of her as his finger had done. Except this time it was even more provoking. A surge of passion unleashed in her and an orgasm tore through her body at an earth-shattering rate. Her loud panting and calling out of his name had to have broken the sound barrier. She was drenched in sweat and the aftermath trembles shook her body more as he never let up his pace. He clinched her butt hard as her hips began to rotate in the same manner as his tongue. She felt helpless with no control of her body's spasms or the unrecognizable sounds she made as she coasted into ecstasy.

The hardness of the desk on her back was erased, and she felt herself drifting on something pillowy. She sighed as her breathing returned to a normal pace and she opened her eyes. She was in a daze but still floating as she smiled and looked up into Broderick's eyes as he hovered over. Touching his face, she gave a lazy smile.

"Hi, beautiful. Are you okay?"

"I'm perfect. You're perfect." She moved her head to the side, expecting to see the cherrywood paneling but instead she saw a rich gold wallpaper. "Where are we?"

"In my bedroom. You fell asleep after that last orgasm so I brought you in here to rest."

Sitting up, she glanced around the enormous room and then looked down at herself. She was relieved to see that she was still fully clothed. "How long have I been out?"

"Not long. Maybe twenty minutes." He reached over to the nightstand and grabbed a bottle of water.

She was dehydrated after all the panting and took a long swig. "Oh my goodness… I've never passed out after an orgasm, but then again no one has ever done what you just did."

Broderick frowned. "You mean the orgasm part, right?"

"No, I mean you kissing me there."

His face was a ball of confusion. "Huh?"

"The only man I've ever been intimate with was Keith, and he never wanted to do that."

"Why the hell not? That's like a woman not wanting to eat chocolate. It's simply unheard of. He must not have known how delectably sweet you are. Damn, the brother missed out, but I'm glad I had the first taste."

"On another note, how long have we been away from your guests?"

"Mmm…about two hours." He shrugged with an uncaring expression.

"Broderick, that's a long time."

He stood and grabbed his black mask from the nightstand. "I freshened up while you rested and I placed your things in the bathroom. Feel free to use whatever. I'll head back down and mingle for a bit and come get you in about twenty minutes."

"I'll be here," she answered with a smirk. She couldn't believe she was actually in his bed because she'd fallen asleep from an orgasm. She could just see Megan and Syd laughing outright if she ever told them.

Later on that night as Tiffani finally rested in her

own bed, she couldn't help but think about her evening with Broderick. The things that man did with his tongue were unreal. She still couldn't believe she was being in the moment with one of the nicest men she'd ever met. He wasn't arrogant or cocky as some men were with their wealth. If he was those things, he wasn't with her. She was glad she had confided in him about her marriage and her theory on relationships and that they were on the same page.

Even though she didn't know what direction her life was taking, she was still happy and in control of her own decisions.

Chapter 6

"Girl, I so needed this," Megan said, pouring a glass of wine. "You want white zin or the merlot?" she asked Tiffani, who was stepping into the room carrying a tray of chocolate raspberry tarts that were fresh out of the oven.

The ladies had convened in the Paint, Sip, Chat next door to Tiffani's bakery for a family night of fun and catching up while testing out their artistic sides. She set her tray on the snack table next to the Thai chicken wings and the spinach dip with pita bread that Megan had brought.

"I'll wait until Preston arrives with the margarita mix. Is something up with you?" Tiffani asked, concerned. She then sat next to Megan at a long table set up with six painting stations of easels, canvases, paint and brushes with white smocks draped over the back of the chairs.

"I just needed a break. Luckily, *The Best Decorated Homes* is on hiatus until January and I can concentrate on my clients here in Atlanta. However, Devin is breaking ground soon on a lakefront subdivision in North Carolina and wants my team to decorate the five model homes. We're studying the floor plans, trying to come up with concepts and designs. So yes, I'm glad you arranged this outing. My brain needed a rest from fabrics and furnishings."

"Well, painting, along with a good glass of wine, can be relaxing."

"Hey, ladies," Preston greeted, strolling in with a wide smile and a box containing a blender, tequila, small bag of ice and margarita mix. He peered around the room at the paintings and murals on the walls. "Whose idea was it to come here and paint? All I can draw is stick people."

"It was mine, big bro." Tiffani jumped up and kissed his cheek. "I thought it would be fun."

He chuckled and plugged in the blender. "Well, next time I'll nominate paintball or dirt bike racing. Sydney and I would enjoy that much more. Who are we waiting for?"

"The newlyweds and Braxton," Megan answered. "The senator is in DC."

Tiffani looked up to see Sydney and Bryce trek in

carrying their motorcycle helmets. "Isn't it too cold to ride your motorcycles? It's forty degrees tonight."

A wicked smirk lit Sydney's face. "Not when we ride together on the same bike, and especially not when I'm driving." She winked and slid her black leather jacket off. Bryce popped her leather-clad bottom with his hand and headed over to chat with Preston.

Tiffani laughed. "I hear you, girl. Help yourself to some food and drinks. Our session begins in a few moments and the instructor will be in soon."

Tiffani's cell phone beeped in her jeans pocket. As she pulled it out and glanced at it, a huge grin etched across her face when she saw a short text from Broderick. For a moment she forgot that she wasn't alone in the room. The text simply read "Take pics." She couldn't help but giggle because she always requested him to take pictures and he'd grunt but would occasionally send one. This was the first time he'd asked for one. Tiffani had invited him to attend the painting party, but he'd declined, citing a meeting. In a way she was relieved. When she'd asked him it was on a whim just to see what he would say.

"What has you so giggly lately?" Megan asked. "I should start calling you Ms. Giggles. You laughed and texted all day when we went shopping on Sunday. Is there something you're not telling us?"

The room fell silent and all eyes were now on Tiffani. She wasn't ready to discuss Broderick just yet with the group. Sure, they all knew him except for Preston, but she didn't know how to explain their relationship status. Whatever it was worked for them, and she was satisfied.

"What's up, fam?" Braxton announced, striding in with a covered tray. "The chef at the club just made these delicious sweet potato fries, so eat up. I figured they'd go great with Megan's wings." He stopped and noticed everyone eyeing Tiffani. "Why is everyone staring at Tiff?" he asked with an amused smirk.

"I don't know Braxton. Now that you're here, we can begin. I'll let the instructor know we're ready." Grateful for the escape, she skedaddled out of the private studio and into the next one, where their instructor, Blythe, was checking on another group.

When Tiffani returned, jazz played low in the background. A tune she was sure Braxton had written. Owner of the hottest jazz club in Atlanta, Café Love Jones, he was also an accomplished jazz pianist and songwriter.

"All right, we can begin," Tiffani announced, putting on her smock and plopping in her seat. "All eyes on Blythe."

"Yes, indeed," she heard Preston whisper as a half smile inched up the left side of his mouth. He then sat down next to Tiffani and set a plate of food between them to share. She thumped her brother playfully on the knee as he gazed lustfully at the instructor. Blythe was indeed an attractive young woman with a thick mane of hair cornrowed on her scalp but loose on the ends, which were pulled into a ponytail on top of her head. She wore a tie-dyed T-shirt cinched at her belly button, which was pierced with a diamond navel ring, black jeans with rips at the knees and a pair of jeweled flip-flops. She reminded Tiffani of the singer Alicia Keys when her first album was released with her bohemian style of dress and was the cool, down-to-earth girl guys wanted to hang out with.

"Hola, everyone," she started in her raspy, deep voice. "I'm Blythe Ventura, owner of Paint, Sip, Chat and that's what I want everyone to do this evening. It doesn't matter if you actually know how to paint or not. It's about having fun with your family." She glanced around the room. "I believe everyone has been here before except for two new faces. Please tell me your name, and if you have any questions feel free to ask." Her eyes lingered on Preston for a second and then shot to Braxton.

"I'm Braxton Chase, Megan and Syd's big brother. I've been looking forward to catching up with my family. With my hectic schedule, I don't always have a chance to hang."

"Nice to finally meet you. I've been to your club a few times. Love the jazz and the food. You're a monster on the keys." Blythe turned her attention to Preston. "And you, sir?"

"Sir? I like that. I'm Preston Chase, Tiff's big brother. I can honestly say I can't paint so I may need a little extra help tonight with a few things, like which way to stroke the paintbrush and what position to hold it in. You know, however you prefer it, Blythe."

Tiffani glanced at Blythe, who simply said "no problem" and continued with her instructions. If she was ruffled by Preston she definitely didn't let it show. Women usually flirted back with him and sometimes first if they were bold enough. He was the pretty-boy type with silk curls, flawless butterscotch skin and a clean-shaven face; sometimes he would sport a mustache and goatee. Plus, he was one of Atlanta's hottest and richest bachelors, having made his fortune from creating video games for smart phones and tablets. Of course, he always loved a challenge and Tiffani sighed when she figured the next two hours would be long if he decided to flirt with Blythe…who wasn't paying him any attention.

"So is everyone ready to see what you're painting tonight?" Blythe asked, standing next to an easel in the front of the room with a white sheet draped over it.

"A naked woman? Preferably y…" Preston stopped as Tiffani pinched him on the knee. He'd whispered the last part, so she hoped Blythe didn't hear him.

"No, Preston, it's not me if that's what you were going to say," Blythe commented as she slid the sheet off of the easel to reveal a painting of a tree with fall leaves and a pumpkin at the bottom with different-colored leaves scattered about. "I figured this would be unisex, and considering it's almost Thanksgiving, this would be perfect. Go ahead and study it…"

Tiffani's concentration was interrupted by her cell phone vibrating in her pocket. She really didn't want to pull it out, but it could be the babysitter. This wasn't her first painting party so she already knew the instructions. She excused herself outside to the yellow-and-pink-striped bench that sat between her bakery and Paint, Sip, Chat. Once seated, she pulled out the phone and was elated to see a text from Broderick that had asked if the painting session had started. As she was typing her answer wearing a Cheshire cat smile, he sent another text.

Goodness, you're beautiful.

Heat rose to her cheeks and she swiped her hand through her hair. As Tiffani tried to quickly finish her message about the session so she could jet back inside, she heard the click of shoes walking her way and then stop. She glanced up a tad to see black men's dress shoes as the enticing scent of cologne she knew all too well drifted to her nose. Slowly, she lifted her eyes and they met the hypnotizing stare of Broderick Hollingsworth in all of his alluring sexiness.

"Well, isn't this a pleasant surprise?" Although she was delighted to see him, she didn't know what to say to her family if he were there to paint after all.

"My meeting ended earlier than expected and because it wasn't far from here, I decided to drop by since you did invite me."

"Of course." She raked her eyes over him and stood up from the bench. "You have to take all this off."

Drawing her to him, he lowered his lips to hers, kissing her tenderly. "So we're going to make love for the first time on the bench outside of your bakery. Nice." Sliding his coat off, he tossed it on the bench and wrapped his hands around her waist again while walking them backward. "You can sit on it," he teased. "And I'll start out by doing that one thing you love."

She gave his chest a gentle push before she followed his exact suggestion. The simple kiss rippled fire straight to her core and now she yearned for him to kiss her again and do that one thing that made her unconscious. "Ha-ha. I meant, you're overdressed. You just need your shirt and pants. Actually, just a casual shirt and jeans would've been fine."

"All right, but I like my idea better." He winked and took off his suit jacket and tie.

The notion of them making love was now clouding her brain. Her vivid thoughts were further enhanced when he unbuttoned the top two buttons of his shirt as they strolled into the lobby of the paint studio. She'd never gotten the chance to plant kisses all over him and now that he was showing a small portion of his chest she longed to sample it.

"I think you know everyone except for my cousin Braxton and my brother...Preston." Dang it. She'd forgotten all about her brother. Every since she'd told him about Keith's treatment of her, Preston had been a real ass toward any man she'd brought around.

"I know Braxton. I've been to a few events at his club, and he's played at some of my private parties."

"Great. Just be yourself." Tiffani mustered up all the strength she had as they headed down the hallway to their private room. Taking a deep breath, she twisted the doorknob and entered with Broderick towering over her by her side.

"Do we have room for one more?" she asked with a nervous laugh.

She locked eyes with Preston as he held his paintbrush in midair with Blythe leaning over him. Everyone seemed to be in midst of something. Syd held her wineglass just at the tip of her lips but wasn't drinking and Megan was in the middle of talking, or maybe she was simply in shock because her mouth was wide open.

Blythe strolled to a shelf and gathered more supplies. "Of course. There's always room for one more. Let me grab you a smock and an easel."

"Who's your friend?" Preston asked in a firm, deep voice.

Tiffani cleared the frog stuck in her throat. "I believe most of you know Broderick Hollingsworth."

Bryce rose and gave Broderick a handshake. "What's up, man?"

"Hey, what's up? Missed you and Syd at my Halloween party, but I know you had the event at the community center for the children."

"Yeah, it was a great night for the kids. They had a lot of fun. How was your party?"

"Oh…it was the best one I've had. Tiffani even stopped by."

She relaxed a tad because Bryce was friends with Broderick. The two carried on their conversation as Preston eyed her. Once Blythe set up the empty station on the other side of Tiffani, they sat down and started to catch up with everyone else working on the background of the painting.

Everyone was silent as they painted, ate and sipped wine or margaritas. Tiffani caught Megan, who was sitting across from her, peer over the easel with a raised eyebrow and a twinkle in her eye. Ever since she'd met and fallen in love with US Senator Steven Monroe three years ago and married him a year later, Megan had wanted the same for her loved ones.

"So, how did y'all meet, *Tiffani*?" Preston asked, sipping on his margarita and setting the glass down with a hard bam.

"At Syd's wedding." *Oh boy. Here we go. Please don't embarrass me.*

"Oh yeah, I do remember seeing you two chat briefly. I had no idea you were now dating."

"We're just friends, Prez. That's it." She bit into a sweet potato fry and hoped that was the end of Preston's questions. After all, she'd said they weren't dating. Which wasn't actually a lie.

"I see. What happened to that other dude I met earlier this summer at the hardware store when we were looking at fixtures for your kitchen and bathroom? He seemed eager to tag along with us."

"Mmm…you scared him away with all of your questions," she answered sarcastically. "And the drill you kept playing with."

"Right. By the way, I see—or, rather, smell—that you're wearing that perfume again. You know, the one that smells like cologne."

Tiffani didn't answer Preston but instead continued painting the trunk of the tree. Her brother never missed a beat and remembered everything. He'd been like that growing up. Always paying attention to every minute detail, which was probably why he was one of the top video game creators, but at times it racked her nerves.

He quieted down but Tiffani knew it would start again. Maybe not that evening, but he'd want to know more eventually.

"Soooooooooo…" Megan began as she glanced at Tiffani with a reassuring smile. "I wanted to know what are everyone's plans for Thanksgiving this year? I spoke to my parents and they're going to Memphis to spend the holidays with Aunt Darla and the Arrington crew, so no dinner at my parents' home this year. Does anyone have any other suggestions?"

Tiffani raised her paintbrush and was grateful to her cousin for the change of subject. "My parents are going on a cruise Thanksgiving week so I don't mind volunteering to host if everyone brings a dish. KJ has been begging me to have Thanksgiving dinner at our house."

"That's a great idea," Megan answered. "Is that all right with the group?"

Everyone else nodded or said yes. They continued painting as Syd and Bryce discussed their motorcycle honeymoon adventure through Bermuda. Tiffani wasn't listening as she sat numbly between Preston and Broderick. She tried to concentrate on painting the pumpkin like a cupcake because Blythe had suggested for everyone to show their own personal creative sides or interests. Preston was undoubtedly quiet. However, she did catch him stealing glances at Blythe as she browsed around at everyone's masterpieces.

"Broderick, what are you doing for the holidays?" she asked, remembering he didn't have a family to spend the holidays with. The thought made her sad for him. She couldn't fathom not being in contact with her family.

"Um…haven't decided. I usually go skiing or to a beach resort. I honestly hadn't thought about it. There are a lot of business deals on my plate right now so my mind has been on those and a few other distractions." He lightly bumped his shoe on hers, and she almost painted a crooked leaf on the pumpkin cupcake.

"What do you do for a living, man?" Preston asked, dipping his paintbrush in water and staring over Tiffani's head to Broderick.

Setting his paintbrush down, Broderick looked at

Preston and smiled. "I'm a real estate investor, but I dabble in other things, as well. What about you?"

"I create video games. Started out with a major company and now I have my own. Perhaps you've heard of Dart and Drive? You can download it for free to all cell phones, tablets and computers. I have others, but that's the most popular one."

"I've heard of it," Broderick said, rubbing his beard. "Not really into children's games, but I hear that industry does well. Perhaps I should look into it."

"I don't have any complaints," Preston said before looking directly at her. "Sis, have you heard any news about the selling of this shopping center?"

"No, Prez, but Blythe and I are trying to stay positive."

Broderick patted her knee. "That's the best thing to do. Remember I told you those type of business transactions take time, precious."

She almost choked on the air in her windpipe when he said "precious." She remained frozen for a moment as she waited for Preston to say something...but he didn't. However, she did sense him staring at her out of the corner of his eye.

They painted and discussed the menu for Thanksgiving and who was bringing what dish for the next hour until everyone was finished with their artwork. Blythe took pictures for her website before leaving to begin her last group of the evening in the next room. They all bid each other good night and walked to their cars. Before Megan left, she mouthed "call me" to Tiffani as she unlocked the door to her bakery to grab her belongings. Broderick hadn't left her side, and now he sat at the counter while she ran to her office to grab her purse and jacket. When she returned he was eyeing their paintings, which were propped on one of the tables side by side.

"We did a great job," he said. "Trying to think where I can hang mine."

"I don't think it goes with your décor."

"Yeah, you're right and Megan spent so much energy and time decorating, I'd hate to mess up the theme of the house. I believe she said it was 'old world meets contemporary' or something like that. I'll find another place to hang it." He shrugged and slid off the bar stool. "I had fun. Thanks for inviting me."

"I'm glad you came. I'm sorry Preston was a jerk."

"Nope, it's understandable. He doesn't want anyone to hurt his baby sister the way your late husband did. He went a little easy I think since I'm cool with Bryce and Braxton. But I'm sure Preston will grill them about me eventually."

"You are so right. Can you walk me to my car? I have to relieve the babysitter in twenty minutes."

"Of course."

He stepped outside while she set the alarm and locked the doors.

They walked in silence to her car. She wanted to ask him again about Thanksgiving since he had never really answered her. She knew he didn't have any family, or least not any he was in contact with, and according to him, his friends were mostly business associates. They stopped at her driver's-side door and, looking up at him, she grabbed his hand. She didn't want him to be alone.

"So if you're not traveling this year for Thanksgiving, you can spend it with me and my family. You know practically all of us."

"Mmm…wow. I can't remember the last time I spent Thanksgiving with a family. How about I let you know really soon. You do know that means I'll have to meet KJ. Are you ready for that?"

She pondered for a moment and reached up and kissed him deeply on the lips. "Yes. I think he'll like you. You should meet him soon."

"No problem. Just let me know when." He opened her door and she slid into the seat, placing her picture on the passenger side and tossing her purse in the back.

"Drive safe. Oh wait. You didn't drive," she joked.

"Actually I did." He kissed her forehead and walked off in the direction of a red Ferrari. "Good night, beautiful," he called out and her heart hammered hard against her chest. She couldn't help it. She was falling for him and she prayed that KJ would like him, too.

Chapter 7

"Long day." Blythe yawned as she entered the bakery and plopped onto the window seat. "Tiffy, please tell me you made something with chocolate that's gluten free. I thought surely I smelled it through the walls and the paint fumes."

Grabbing her tongs and a napkin, Tiffani opened the case and snatched a cream-cheese brownie. "You're in luck. I have one left." She strolled over to her friend and handed it to her.

Blythe bit into it and sighed. "Heaven. Girl, put it on my tab."

Tiffani pounced on the little bean bag in front of the bookcase that KJ had insisted be placed there. "What's wrong?"

"Just a little worried about the possibility of losing my business, or at least this location. Things are really great over there and over here, too. I really want to hire another assistant, but what if I need that money to relocate?" Biting into the brownie, she exhaled.

"Girl, I hear you. It's just me, Kendall and Mindy but I've thought about that, as well."

"Well, I have a friend who said he'll do some digging around. You know these investors like to be secretive so that other ones in their circle won't know what they're doing. If I hear anything I'll let you know."

"Thanks, hon."

"Aren't you dating a real estate investor?"

"We aren't calling it that. We're just…"

"I know, I know. You're being in the moment or whatever," Blythe teased. "I do like the idea. I've been celibate for so long maybe I should just *be* in the moment, myself."

"It think that's what you're doing, except by yourself."

Both ladies laughed as Tiffani walked to the door and locked it. It was officially closing time. She turned the lighted open sign off and retreated to finish counting the contents of the cash register.

"Tiffani, you're crazy. That's probably why I need all this dang chocolate."

"I completely understand. But getting back to the topic at hand—Broderick has told me it's a long process. So in the meantime, I'm saving a little extra when

I can and I've started researching other locations I may want to consider if I have to relocate."

"I'd hate to have to move. This is a great area. I've been here for two years and business is wonderful. I can always go back to teaching art in a high school, but I prefer what I'm doing now."

"I hear you. I did enjoy teaching as well, but I love what I'm doing now, too. I'm my own boss…even though I miss having the summers off."

"That was always a plus."

Tiffani pondered on something she'd wanted to ask Blythe since the paint party. "So what do you think about Preston?"

Blythe pursed her lips to hold in a laugh that stumbled out anyway. "Girl, please. I know his type. No offense."

Tiffani shrugged. "None taken. I know my brother, and he's a straight-up player. I just liked the way you remained professional and didn't lose your cool when he was clearly flirting and eyeing you the entire time. He's used to women flirting back and chasing him."

"Well, there's definitely no chase with me," Blythe said, shaking her head. "However, your cousin Braxton is quite handsome. You know I like chocolate, and he's bald." She popped the last of the brownie in her mouth. "A great combination."

"Yeah, he's a good guy. A little eccentric at times but he's a musical genius. He gets so wrapped up in his music that sometimes life passes him by. That's how he lost the love of his life. Anyway, I wouldn't dare hook you up with my brother. I just liked the way you handled him."

Blythe stood and straightened her Aztec maxi skirt. "Yeah. I'm kind of used to doing that when single men come to the studio. He was just having fun. I didn't take him seriously." She shrugged and smiled. "I have one more paint party tonight and then I'm going home to soak in the hot tub."

"Okay, chica. Have fun. I'm leaving here to pick up KJ from my parents' house. He's meeting Broderick for the first time, and I'm nervous. I may need some chocolate, too!"

"KJ, remember when Mommy told you that I went to my friend Mr. Hollingsworth's home for a Halloween party while you were at the sleepover?" she asked as she backed out of her parents' driveway. She glanced at KJ in the rearview mirror before shifting the car in drive.

"Oh, yeah," KJ answered as he played a video game that Preston had given him to test out. "Glad you had fun, Mom," KJ said, clearly distracted.

"I did. He knows Uncle Bryce and Auntie Syd. He was at their wedding. That's where I met him."

"Uh-huh. You already told me, Mom."

She glanced at him again, but he was so into the game he was barely listening.

"Mr. Hollingsworth has invited us out for bowling and pizza tonight." She tried to keep her voice steady.

She didn't know why she was so nervous, but then again, she'd never introduced KJ to a man she was spending time with before.

"Who else will be there?"

"Um…just the three us."

He tore his attention away from his game and met her eyes in the mirror. "But you can't bowl, Mommy."

She laughed. "No, but you know how to and so does Mr. Hollingsworth."

"Are you dating him?"

She pondered on that. Dating wasn't in her vocabulary, but she wasn't going into a long explanation with an eight year old about her "be in the moment" theory. "Um…we're good friends and we hang out. Talk on the phone."

"I'll meet him, but I can't make any promises that I'll like him."

"Fair enough."

As they pulled into the parking lot, Tiffani spotted Broderick's Ferrari and parked next to it.

"Nice ride," KJ stated as they walked by it.

"That's Mr. Hollingsworth's car."

"Cool. He has good taste in cars."

Once they entered the bowling alley, Tiffani scanned the facility until her eyes landed on Broderick sitting in one of the lane areas. Her heart fluttered as he waved them over, and she was elated to finally see him dressed down in casual khakis with a blue polo shirt and deck shoes.

"That's him, Mom?" KJ asked.

"Yep."

"He doesn't look anything like my father," KJ said, shaking his head with a pout.

Tiffani abruptly stopped in her tracks and looked down at her son. "Why did you think he would look like your father?"

"Because Grandmother Lake said if you ever dated or remarried you would probably find someone just like Dad because he's all you've ever known and that you'd want somebody just like him to fill a void."

Not in this lifetime, buddy. Not ever.

"She told you that?"

"No. I overheard her talking to some of her bridge club friends."

"Oh, well let's go meet Mr. Hollingsworth."

Out of respect for Keith's parents after he died, Tiffani never told them how horrible and controlling he'd been to her during their marriage. He'd been a loyal and devoted son to them, and she didn't want to tarnish their image of him.

"Hello, Tiffani," Broderick said, reaching out and giving her a slight hug. They'd agreed beforehand to just keep it light and casual around KJ. "And who is this handsome young man? Your bodyguard?"

"I'm Keith Jonathan Lake Jr., but everyone calls me KJ." He held out his hand to Broderick, who shook it.

"You have a tight grip there, sport." Broderick caught eyes with Tiffani and winked. "I'm Broderick Jerold

Hollingsworth. I don't have a nickname, though. You think I need one?"

KJ tapped his chin. "Mmm…how about Mr. H?"

Broderick nodded and smiled. "I like that. So your mother tells me you bowl quite well."

"Yes. My Uncle Preston and my grandpa taught me."

"Cool. Let's go get you some shoes. Tiffani, we'll be back."

An hour and a half later, KJ was dancing and cheering in the lane area. He'd just defeated Broderick for the second time. Broderick pretended to be upset, and challenged him to a rematch at a later date. Tiffani was glad they were getting along. She liked Broderick more than she cared to admit, and because they were hanging out more now, she wanted KJ to like him, as well.

They decided to eat at the bowling alley's restaurant because KJ liked the root beer floats they served. Tiffani and Broderick waited in their booth for the food while watching KJ play on the pinball machine a few feet away.

"So what's the verdict? You think he likes me?" Broderick asked, as he nodded toward KJ and sipped his soda.

"I believe so, especially since you let him win two games in a row."

Broderick shrugged his shoulders. "I just wanted him to have fun, but he's really good. I was actually trying to win in the second game, but I messed up twice. I was distracted by the lady in the sexy jeans and boots. Next time, you can't come."

The food arrived, and KJ returned, sliding into the booth next to his mother.

"Wait," Tiffani started as KJ's hands reached for his burger basket on the tray. "You two need hand sanitizer." She opened her tote bag and pulled out a Ziploc bag.

"Ah, Mom. Mr. H and I are men. We're tough." KJ rolled up his shirt sleeve and showed his little muscles.

"And so are the nasty germs that have been all over those bowling balls." She squirted the sanitizer into both their hands and then hers.

They began to eat as KJ discussed his day at school and an upcoming science fair project. Broderick seemed to take an interest and asked questions about his grades and classmates.

"I think I like you, Mr. H. The next time we all go out, I'll teach you some of my karate moves so you can protect Mommy when I'm not with her."

Tiffani almost choked on her French fry and glanced at Broderick, who had an amused expression on his face.

"I look forward to that, young man. I definitely wouldn't want anything to happen to your mom when you aren't there to protect her. I'll definitely need to learn some karate moves. She tells me you've won awards. That's outstanding."

"Thanks. Hey, I know you were just letting me win in bowling. You did well. You have the proper form, like Uncle Preston. He says I'm getting there. He taught me how to bowl since my father is in heaven. Did your father teach you how to bowl?"

"No, he wasn't around much when I was growing up, but you're fortunate to have your grandfathers and uncles to teach you those things."

"Is your daddy in heaven, too?" KJ asked with a solemn face.

"No, he's here in Atlanta."

"Do you go bowling together now?"

Tiffani wiped her mouth with her napkin. "KJ, that's enough questions. Finish your fries. It's getting late."

Broderick shook his head. "No, Tiff I don't mind. KJ, my dad and I aren't close. However, a dear friend of mine recently suggested that I go see him, and I've been considering that more and more lately. I think hanging with you tonight has helped me make a final decision."

"That's good, Mr. H. I'm sure he'd be happy to see you."

Nodding, a genuine smile formed on his face. "Thanks, kiddo. I'll let you know how it goes."

"You can take pictures." KJ slurped the rest of his root beer float and placed the empty cup on the tray.

Broderick laughed out loud and stood to gather all of their trash on the tray. "You sound like your mother," he said as he turned with the tray. "I'm going to go toss this."

"So you like Mr. H, huh?" Tiffani asked, relieved that the two were getting along well.

"Yep, Mom. He's cool. I hope he and his dad make up since he's still alive."

"Me, too. Now let's go. I have to be at the bakery early in the morning, and I've noticed you stifle about five yawns. Grab your video game player and your jacket."

Moments later, Broderick walked Tiffani and KJ to her car.

"It was great meeting you, young man," Broderick said, holding the car door open for KJ.

"You, too, Mr. H." He gave Broderick a high-five and jumped in the backseat and began to play his game again.

"Well, I had fun, Tiff. He's a great kid. You've raised him well."

"Thank you. I've had a lot of help." She looked up at him and ran her hand down his face. "I'm glad you're going to go see your father."

He kissed the inside of her palm and then squeezed it. "I think it's time." He opened her car door. "Be safe. Call me when you get home, beautiful."

She beamed at his words. She loved when he used terms of endearment. It reminded her of all the pet names her father called her mother. Tiffani was glad a man was finally doing so with her.

Tiffani leaned over the counter at the bakery while perusing the internet. KJ was spending the upcoming weekend with his paternal grandparents, and she was searching for a quick getaway. In talking with Blythe

the other day about summer vacations, she realized she hadn't had her usual break this past summer. She had opened her bakery in June, after having worked on it since April. KJ had the pleasure of spending two weeks in Europe with her parents on his last summer break. Because they were retired, her parents traveled often.

The bakery currently was empty. A water pipe had burst a few blocks up, which had flooded the main road, and traffic had been rerouted away from the shopping plaza. A couple of regular customers had straggled in that morning for their usual Danishes and stuffed croissants, but for the most part business had been slow for a Tuesday.

The sound of the bell on the door brought her out of vacation search. A surprised smile emerged on her face as Broderick casually strode in wearing a delicious grin.

"You know leaning over like that can get you in trouble, woman." Reaching over the counter he popped her bottom, causing her to laugh. "Whatcha doing?"

"Searching for a getaway. Somewhere nearby, no more than five hours away because I'm driving."

"For spring break?" He sat on one of the bar stools as his eyes glanced at the goodies in the display case.

"For this weekend. KJ is spending it with the Lakes, you know, my-in-laws. Kendall and Mindy can run the bakery on Friday and Saturday. I'm hoping to leave Thursday evening after dropping him off once I figure out where I'm going."

"Oh…you're going alone?"

She placed her eyes on him for a moment and then back at the screen. "You can come with me...once I decide where I'm going," she answered sarcastically. Her heart dropped. Had she just asked the man to spend the weekend with her? That had never been her intention, but now she hoped he'd say yes because the sensual image that had just appeared in her mind needed to be a reality. Ever since he'd mentioned them making love on the bench that'd been all she could think about.

"Unfortunately, I can't. I have meetings all day on Friday and an event on Saturday evening. I was going to ask if you wanted to come with me, but you do need a vacation."

She was disappointed. Now she didn't want to go away, but this was her only chance, and she could use some relaxation. "Yes, I do. The next two weeks are going to be hectic with orders for Thanksgiving parties."

"You know, I own a vacation house on Tybee Island. You're more than welcome to use it. It's only a four-hour drive from here and it's free."

Her ears perked up when she heard the word *free*. "Really? I haven't been there since I was a teenager."

"It's yours for the weekend. Just let me know so I can have the rental management company make sure everything is ready for you. Would you like a personal chef?"

She waved her hands in front of her. "Slow down, Broderick. I don't need all that."

"Or I have a place in the Florida Keys. You can lie out on the beach all day."

"I can't drive to the keys. Tybee is fine, even though the Keys sounds wonderful."

"I have a private jet. It can take you down there and then a helicopter can take you to the island."

"The island?"

"It's a private one. I own it. Very secluded. Only my house is it on it."

She laughed nervously. "Broderick, that's too much for the weekend. I'll just go to the one on Tybee."

"Nonsense. You deserve it. It's on me." He jumped off the bar stool. "I need to run, but I'll have everything set up for you on Thursday evening. I'll have Leslie call you with the details."

"I didn't agree to the Keys."

He closed the lid of her laptop. "It's a done deal." He pointed his finger on the glass display. "Let me have one of those Snickers brownies and we're even."

"I don't think a three-dollar Snickers brownie will make up for a jet and a private island for the weekend."

"Fine. Throw in a picture of you lying out on the beach in your bikini."

Laughing, she placed two brownies in a box and handed it to him. "Fine, and since it's a secluded island I can take it off afterward and sunbath naked. Yep, this vacation is going to be awesome. No tan lines."

Wearing a sinfully delicious smile he tilted his head

to the side and his eyes darkened. "Naked? I may have to cancel my plans and come with you."

"I wish you could."

He leaned over the counter and kissed her deeply as her eyes fluttered shut at its impact. A loud gasp escaped her, but he meshed his mouth on hers even more, which muffled her passionate moans. Circling his tongue uncontrollably with hers, he held her face firmly in his hands while she tried not to stumble over the counter.

"I'm about to fall."

"Me, too," he whispered on her lips. "Fall forever."

Jerking her eyes open, she pulled back. She was grateful the counter was between them and that the bakery was open because she wanted him at that very moment. Even though she'd meant literally fall on the floor, the way he said it turned her skin ablaze and her heart had skipped a few beats.

His stare was hazy as he raked his eyes over her before swiping the box from the counter. "Well, I need to get going. I'm hopping on the jet in an hour to look at some lakefront property in North Carolina that I'm considering investing in. In fact, Megan and her design team are already down there."

"Oh, Devin Montgomery's new subdivision. Megan told me about it briefly at the painting party before you arrived." She was glad they'd skipped to another topic before she closed the bakery, gave Mindy the day off and dragged him to her office to finish their kiss. No, finish their escapade from the night of his party. She still experienced ardent tremors from that night.

"You know Devin?"

"Not really. His fiancée, Sasha Monroe, is Bryce and Steven's cousin, and I've seen them a few times this year. She's asked me to do their wedding cakes."

He nodded as if he'd barely heard a word she'd said. "You know, I keep replaying the first time I laid eyes on you and how you glided so eloquently down the aisle. Goodness you were beautiful and sexy as hell. Graceful. I stared at you the entire time. I don't remember the wedding…just you. I thought you were the epitome of what I've been searching for in a woman. I was think…"

The bell ringing on the door jolted both their heads to turn to in its direction as a couple of women with baby strollers and two toddlers entered.

"Welcome to Sweet Treats," Tiffani greeted in a voice that had gone up an entire octave.

Broderick's assessment of her had sent her pulse speeding and tiny beads of sweat had formed on her forehead. She didn't have time to process it all as the customers placed their order and she began setting their treats in boxes while trying to keep her hand steady. However, his last sentence continued to play in her head louder than one of the toddlers who had begun to cry because his mother said he could only pick one cupcake. Tiffani glanced up while ringing the ticket and looked right into Broderick's smoldering stare as he stood near the door. He took out his cell phone, typed something and walked out of the door. Seconds later, her cell phone vibrated in her apron pocket. She knew it was from him and she was itching to read it as her heart pounded. Once her customers settled in the front booth by the window, she skated to the kitchen, where Mindy was icing cupcakes for an order that evening.

"Mindy, I need to make a really important phone call. Can you go out front for about twenty minutes? You can take the tray of cupcakes with you."

"Sure thing, boss."

"Thanks."

Tiffani rushed back to her office, closed the door and leaned on it. Taking a deep breath, she pulled her phone from her apron and pressed the home screen button. His text was a continuation of what he was saying before the customers entered.

I was thinking the man who ends up with her will be a lucky son of a gun. For a moment, I actually got a little jealous because I wanted it to be me and I still do.

Sighing, she headed to her desk and tossed the phone on it. She'd been afraid something like this would happen, but deep down she wanted the same Broderick did. She knew in heart and soul she was falling for him. And now that she had, she wasn't going to stop.

Chapter 8

Tiffani stared out the window of the Lincoln Town Car taking her to the private airfield so she could fly to Broderick's private island. Every time she thought about where she was going and how she was traveling, she had to pinch herself. His secretary had emailed the itinerary the day before and Tiffani couldn't stop glancing at it. Not because she couldn't remember the details but because she was in disbelief. She'd read romance novels similar to what was happening in her current life, but they were filled with super, über-fantasy events that just didn't happen in real life. Well, unless one was a famous, rich celebrity or dating a millionaire like she was. Once the plane arrived at Florida Keys Marathon Airport, a helicopter would take her to Broderick's private island. Because she'd refused the personal chef and housekeeper, the management company that rents the island out had had someone stock the refrigerator with all of Tiffani's favorite foods and drinks as well as make sure there were enough DVDs to keep her entertained. However, a personal valet was on call and was only a boat ride away should she need anything or want to go to the main island to sightsee or shop.

After spiraling down a road she didn't know existed, the car drove into an airplane hangar and her eyes widened as she saw Broderick's private jet. Painted on the side in bold purple was BJH, his initials. Once out of the car, she was greeted by the captain and a flight attendant, who escorted her up the flight of stairs and informed her they would take off soon for the hour-and-a-half flight.

Tiffani gazed around the exquisite aircraft and wasn't surprised at all by its ambience. It screamed success, wealth and Broderick. The oversized beige seats had his initials engraved in each one. The same cherrywood paneling in the study in his mansion lined the main cabin of the plane. There was a wet bar, a sitting area with a couch and a flat-screen television. She noticed one of the seats was slightly bigger than the rest, and she decided to settle there. Tiffani had a feeling it was Broderick's because on the wall next to the chair was a panel with an intercom. She tossed her bag in the seat facing it and slid her feet underneath her.

"Ms. Lake, can I get you anything? Some champagne or wine? Caviar?" The flight attendant, Carol, asked.

"Champagne would be nice."

"There's a small table that comes out from the wall where you're sitting if you need to do any work. That's usually where Mr. Hollingsworth sits to do his."

Work was the furthest thing from her mind. "No need. I intend to sleep the entire flight," she said, trying to muffle a yawn.

Moments later, Carol returned with a glass of champagne and informed Tiffani they'd take off in about ten minutes. Carol then instructed that if she needed anything once they were in flight, all she had to do was press the button on the wall.

Yawning, Tiffani sipped her champagne and placed it in the cup holder in the seat. Grabbing her purse, she retrieved her cell phone and sent Broderick a thank-you text message and a couple of cute pictures of her in his seat. She wanted to call him, but he'd told her earlier he'd be in a meeting during her flight.

Leaning her head back, she closed her heavy eyelids and dozed off. Some moments later the speed of the airplane taking off jarred her from her short nap, and she opened her eyes to a mirage. Wrinkling her forehead and wiping the blurry sleep out of her eyes, Tiffani's mouth dropped when she saw Broderick sitting across from her, gazing at her with an exceptionally seductive smile.

"Am I dreaming?" she asked, hoping she was truly awake.

A sexy smirk crossed his chiseled face. "No, beautiful. You're in my seat."

Laughing, she took off her seat belt, jumped in his lap and placed kisses all over his face. "What a wonderful surprise. You're actually here. What about your meetings?"

"When you're the boss you can make your own schedule. Besides, my business manager can handle all that. I wanted to spend some time with you."

"Perfect. I would've been bored out my mind on that island by myself the entire weekend." Resting her palms on his cheeks, she kissed his lips tenderly as he returned the kiss in a slow, unhurried pace.

"I want you, Tiffani. Right now," he said, sliding his tongue inside of her mouth.

"Me, too, but the flight attendant is just beyond the door."

He chuckled, reminding her he was in control of their present surroundings. "Trust me, she's not coming in unless I call for her."

Tiffani wasn't convinced as she pulled away from him. "Things may get loud and she could hear me."

"Oh, you will get loud, trust me on that. I intend to ravish you like crazy all over this plane and then at the beach house."

An electric shot jolted through her at the thought,

and she lowered her lips to his once more. "Okay, I'll try to be quiet."

He threw his head back in a loud roar of laughter. "Good luck with that. Now enough talk. The flight is only an hour and a few minutes."

Broderick's lips swiftly and seductively captured hers. Drawing her against his hard chest, he gripped his arms around her. She welcomed the taste of his searching tongue on her lips as he dove in even more, causing wave after wave of pure ecstasy to rocket through her veins, awakening a passion she'd never experienced before meeting Broderick. Her heart and soul were wrapped up in their kiss and she thought for sure she would sink into a comatose abyss from the force. He clutched one hand in her thick tresses, enticing her farther into him. Her mouth eagerly parted more to permit the both of them better access. When he lifted them up from the seat, her legs wrapped around his trim waist as he carried them to the couch. He sat down with her still straddling him. Breaking their kiss, he lowered his dark gaze to her shirt and slowly unfastened the buttons.

"Can't you go faster?" she teased.

"I can go very fast, but I don't want to scare you so early on." He winked and proceeded to place light kisses between her breasts. "Front hook. Easy access."

He undid the clasp on her bra as her breasts popped out and he immediately took one into his mouth as she tried to muffle her moan. But there was no use as he used his tongue to explore both breasts, sucking and taunting her nipples, driving her immensely insane.

"I've wanted to taste these since I saw your hard nipples trying to bust out of that pink tank you wore the day I ordered the cupcakes. Were they aching for me? Is that what you wanted that morning? For me to take you in the back and kiss and tug on them like I'm doing now?"

Had he read her mind? That's exactly what she'd wanted. "Don't stop," she moaned out as her head fell backward and almost rested on his knees. He reached his free hand under her hair and caressed the back of her neck. Tiffani couldn't explain the emotions flowing through her thanks to him. He made her feel alive and sexual. Exquisite. Treasured. Beautiful.

At first Tiffani had wanted to take things slow with Broderick, but the aching she had for him she couldn't suppress any longer, and she had no control over her body when it came to him. His skilled tongue on her skin as he teased and kissed her breasts sent treacherous sensations from the tiny hair follicles on her head all the way down to her toes.

"You're so damn perfect, beautiful," he said in a gruff tone that caused an electric current to ascend through her every cell in her body.

The plane dipped for a second, reminding her they weren't on the ground, and she held on to him tightly just in case it happened again. She hated turbulence on planes.

He claimed her mouth once more in a furious, powerful kiss, sucking the breath of out her lungs and making her forget the turbulence, as they created their own. Needing to feel his chest on hers, she broke off their kiss and lifted his polo shirt over his head and tossed it behind them. Her mouth watered at the gorgeous sight of his muscular, bare chest and she pressed her breasts against his as hard as possible.

Broderick grabbed her by the butt, and flipped her over on the couch and pulled her maxi skirt and panties off simultaneously. "I got to have you now."

"Please hurry up," she screeched out, no longer caring who could hear them. She needed this man more than she needed the breath in her body. She reached up to him and unfastened his belt buckle and zipper as fast as possible.

"Aren't you a feisty little thing?" He stood and yanked his pants and boxers down to his ankles and stepped out of them along with his shoes.

Tiffani closed her eyes and reopened them with a gulp. She had no idea how she was going to handle all of what was in front of her, but she wasn't going to tell him that.

"You'll be fine," he said, removing a packet from his wallet and slipping its contents on his very erect rod.

"What are you talking about?" she smiled, trying to laugh off her nervousness mixed with anticipation.

"I saw your eyes widen like saucers. But I'm convinced you're the only woman meant for me, and so far all of our connections have been astounding."

His heated stare raked over her body. Her frame quivered just from that simple gesture as he positioned his body over hers and lowered his lips to hers unhurried. He buried one of his hands into her hair and used the other to gently guide himself inside of her inch by inch. He still kissed her tenderly and kept his eyes on hers the entire time. She sucked in her breath and panted a few times as she tensed up so he'd stop moving.

"Are you okay?" he whispered on her lips.

"I'm fine. Go ahead." She wrapped her legs around him tighter and held on to his face while keeping her eyes steady with his as he continued to sink deeper.

Tiffani twisted her hips as he slid the rest of the way in. Broderick began to move at a slow rhythm. Her muscles clutched around him with every thrust, and the deeper he stroked, the more she clinched. The magnitude of him in her was uncanny and the suppression of her emotions and moans flew out the window. She shuddered and cried out as loud as she needed as he delved into her over and over, rocking her in an untamed passion. She felt suspended in air, not because she was on an airplane, but because she was in his arms. For the moment, she felt caught up in a world only belonging to them. After her first orgasm tore through her wildly, the second one caught her off guard as his thrusts began to become feral and unpredictable. She loved every minute of it until he reached his climax and grabbed her close to him so fast that she gasped out a long wail that matched his.

After a few minutes of lying intertwined with each other, Broderick lifted his head as he continued to calm his breathing. His sweat dripped on to her face and mingled with hers. "I think we're descending."

"What?" She was so out of it she didn't comprehend what he was saying.

"The plane, I believe, will be descending soon. Apparently you didn't hear the captain's announcement over the intercom."

"Oh my goodness." She wrestled out of his embrace and sat all the way up on the couch. "I didn't hear a single word. Too busy trying to breathe again." Her eyes searched the cabin for her clothes. "Do you know where you threw my panties?"

"I got them." He stood and retrieved their clothes. They hurriedly got dressed and returned to their seats. This time he sat in his seat with her legs outstretched across his lap.

"Girl, you just wore a brother out and you said you couldn't handle it."

"I never said that. You just thought that. So does that mean you're done for the night?" she questioned slyly.

Broderick journeyed his hand up her leg and massaged her center through the fabric of her panties. She sighed at his touch as there was still a tingle remaining from her last climax.

"No. That was just a little sample."

A dangerous grin crossed her face. "Bring it on."

"Oh, I will, and welcome to the Mile High Club," he said, patting her inner thigh before pulling her skirt back down as the plane landed.

"Now, once we get to the island, you can introduce me to the beach club, too." *Goodness, am I that inexperienced when it comes to different places to have sex?*

"Mmm-hmm. Oh I intend to introduce you to a lot of different clubs," he said, shifting in his seat.

"Can't wait."

"It's so peaceful out here under the moon and stars. I'm so glad you came. I don't think I would've laid out here alone if you weren't here. I'd be terrified."

They were relaxing on a hammock on the candle-lit veranda off the master bedroom. They'd made love the moment they had stepped into the house. After a long shower together, a midnight dinner and Broderick smoking a cigar, both were completely sated but now neither of them was ready to go to sleep.

Kissing her forehead, he pulled Tiffani closer to him. She wrapped her legs around his and breathed in deeply. He figured she'd be sleepy by now considering she'd been up since the crack of dawn. He puffed on his cigar and blew the smoke away from her.

"Thanks for letting me smoke. A lot of people hate it."

She shrugged. "No problem. I actually like the smell. Cigarettes, no, but the scent of cigars and pipes remind me of my grandfather. He smoked sometimes when he was alive. Usually for special occasions."

"Is your grandmother still alive?"

"Yes. She has a home in Atlanta, but she goes back and forth between there and Memphis so she can visit with all of her children and grandchildren."

"Sounds like you have a big family."

"On my mom's side I don't. She's an only child, but on the Chase side, my grandparents had three children. My dad is the oldest and then the twins Darla and Richard. Uncle Richard is Megan, Syd and Braxton's father. Aunt Darla and her family are in Memphis. She moved there after medical school with her husband, Uncle Francis. They have a medical practice and their children are all doctors, as well. You probably saw them at Sydney's wedding. All of the bridesmaids were my cousins."

"Babe, the only bridesmaid I noticed was you. Goodness you were beautiful and now you're even more radiant and glowing lying here naked in my arms. You know the island is secluded. We can stay naked the entire time, like we're in the Garden of Eden…"

Thumping his chest playfully, she followed it up with a kiss to his neck. "You're a bad boy, Broderick. As tempting as that sounds, I do want to go into town for some shopping and sightseeing. Is that okay? Just for a few hours?"

Her body tensed against his for a second, and he

knew she was still somewhat guarded. "Of course, babe. You don't have to ask me."

"Okay," she answered quietly.

"I'm not controlling, and I would never take away your independence. Now I may be somewhat of a controlling, arrogant ass with my employees but…" he paused and lifted her chin so she could see that he was being honest "…never with you. Personally, I don't care what we do. I just want to relax with you, see your beaming face and kiss your luscious mouth."

"Aww…you're such a sweetie pie." Poking out her lips, she gave him a smooch on the cheek.

"And you give the sweetest kisses, precious."

"It's so peaceful and serene out here, Broderick."

"That's why I bought the place. I wanted somewhere I could escape with no one around. Just me on my own island away from the hustle and bustle. I rarely leave when I come, and I've never brought anyone with me. No staff. No women. Just the birds and me."

"And you don't feel lonely?"

He had to consider that for a moment. He was never lonely. Alone, yes, but by choice. "With the line of work I do sometimes I need to clear my brain from it all. There's always someone in my ear about a deal, and my business manager is always nagging me to hurry up and make a decision. I never do anything on a whim because it's my millions and my name on the line. So sometimes it's nice to get away, fly down here and relax.

Usually once leaving here, my mind is clear and I can go back with a plan of action."

"Do you have some deals on the table now?"

"Yes, the biggest one is with Devin and Supreme Construction. I was really impressed with the land he's about to break ground on. Even Megan and her crew are excited about decorating the model homes. I haven't signed on the dotted line yet. Still negotiating the money aspect. But when I last spoke to my business manager before I boarded the plane, he said everything was on the up and up. He also updated me on some other possible deals he's been researching that I'm not really interested in. It's always good to keep my options open, but for now I'm sticking with the lakefront subdivision and perhaps one more."

"Do you have to keep investing your money?"

Puffing on his cigar, he beamed with joy "No. I could retire tomorrow and live happily ever after on this island with you and KJ."

Broderick froze as the words spilled out of his mouth. He'd said it so naturally and matter-of-factly. Truth was, he could actually see just that. He could envision him and KJ playing football on the beach while a dog ran alongside them. Tiffani would be inside baking cupcakes and making freshly squeezed lemonade and wearing a pink apron and that huge smile that lit up his days brighter than the sun. But she wouldn't be happy. She'd want her family and friends around and her freedom to live her life as she dreamed with her prosperous bakery, her son and her companion or whatever title she'd given him.

Nuzzling his neck, she wrapped her arms tighter around his waist and whispered, "We'd have to compromise."

Shocked that she would even entertain his fantasy, he shifted them on the hammock so they could face each other. "There's a compromise?"

"Of course." She yawned, which caused him to do the same. "Let's go to bed."

"Only if I can make love to you again."

She slid off of the hammock and he followed her back inside the bedroom. She pounced on the bed and pulled him by the shoulders to her as a mischievous grin lined her face. "That's what I meant by let's go to bed, silly."

Chapter 9

The afternoon sun beamed down, as Tiffani rested her head on Broderick's chest as they relaxed naked on the beach. They'd woken up late that morning, cooked breakfast together, then went shopping and sightseeing on the main island. That had been the routine for the past two days. Tomorrow morning they were headed back to Atlanta and the real world. Her thoughts continued to float back to his fantasy of staying on the island forever with her and KJ. Although she knew that was unrealistic, she didn't mind the forever part. She could actually see herself married to Broderick and being happy. That excited and scared her all at the same time. She knew he wasn't anything like Keith, but the thought of being married again felt like a noose around her neck.

Tiffani traced her finger along his washboard abs that she'd had the pleasure of running more than just her hands across. The mere thought aroused her, but she was too exhausted to move. However, he'd been an awesome lover and if he wanted to make love right now she'd do it in a heartbeat. But he was just as tired as she was. He'd snore, wake up for a moment, kiss her forehead and drift back to sleep. She loved the fact that he acknowledged that she was there while he slept. Keith had never been the affectionate type, no matter how hard she tried to make him be. He didn't believe in PDA, so there was never any hand holding, light kisses in public or even a tender arm around her waist. Broderick had done all those things and it was genuine.

Broderick was indeed a wonderful and compassionate lover. Her mind and soul had never been so in sync before during lovemaking. He was aware of her needs and satisfied her to the fullest. No inch on her body had gone unkissed or untouched, and he did it in the most sensual and loving way. She'd feared since Keith's death that she wouldn't be able to open up to another man physically because she'd only been with him. However, she was wrong on so many levels. It was a new awakening. A new passionate experience that she'd never known was possible. Broderick made her feel like a woman. A sexy, desirable woman who held nothing back during their lovemaking. She was determined to let him know just how much she'd craved and yearned for him. A part of her also wanted to make him feel needed and special, as well. She hated that for the most part he was alone in his own world. It sort of surprised her that he'd bought the island to be even more alone and had never brought anyone here before. The thought peeved her and she wanted him to know that she was someone he could trust and depend on.

She placed a gentle kiss to the side of his neck and he stirred with a smile.

"Hey, beautiful." His voice was groggy but she could hear the affection he felt for her in his tone. "Did I fall asleep?"

"Yep. For a few minutes, but you need your rest. You work all the time."

"That's because someone wouldn't let me rest last night. But I'm not complaining one bit." He popped her bare bottom. "Oh, and don't tell Chef Crenshaw, but I love your crepes and homemade biscuits much better. I'll miss them when we return."

"Thank you." She propped her elbow up and put her shades on her head. "I'm sure it won't be the last time I cook for you."

He pulled her on top of him and kissed her softly. "So on some of the weekends KJ spends with his grandparents, you'll spend yours with me?"

"Yes." Returning his kiss, she felt the slight rise of him on her pelvic area as he nibbled on her bottom lip. "And I must say I enjoyed your omelets. Very cheesy, just the way I like it, with lots of spinach and onions. I was surprised you cook since you have your own personal chef."

"You know I wasn't always wealthy. I learned how to cook when I lived in the group home. And believe it or not I sometimes do so now. Like when I come here, I don't bring anyone including staff and a brother has to eat." He sucked on her ear. "You know how much I love to eat."

She cracked a naughty smile. "Yes, I do. And I've enjoyed every second of it."

"I've created a greedy-for-my-tongue monster."

Broderick sat all the way up as she straddled his lap. She wrapped her legs around his waist as he crashed his lips on hers in a hard yet sensual kiss. She couldn't get enough of him and the way he handled her as if he were placed on Earth only to please her just the way she needed.

Tiffani opened her mouth more to allow him adequate access to her tongue. He kissed her with so much vigor that it ruptured stimulating quivers down to her aching sex. She desired to have him inside of her that very moment. Tiffani had never begged her late husband to have sex with her, but Broderick was a different kind of man. He was a man who took his time to make sure every inch of her was satisfied. He was a man who was patient and understanding about her inexperience. Overall he was the only man she could see herself spending the rest of her life with.

"Broderick, please make love to me." She pulled her lips from his and placed them on his neck.

"My pleasure. Just raise up a moment so I can grab a condom from under the pillow."

Stunned, her eyes shot to his. "You brought one with you?"

A dangerous grin swept his face. "Always have to be prepared when I'm around you."

Once he was secured, she slid back into her original position, but this time he was inside of her. He didn't move or deliver any more mind-blowing kisses. Instead, he gazed at her with a hunger in the depths of his eyes. That alone caused shivers to course every cell in her body.

She pushed up fast but back down slow with a slight wiggle of her hips. When she was on top, she could feel his length and thickness in a place she never knew existed, which caused her to orgasm sooner. This time she wanted to savor the moment with him on the beach as the afternoon sun burned hot on her back and his hand clutched her hips.

Broderick tugged on her breasts, circling his tongue around them as she moved up and down on him at a steady, comfortable pace. She gasped as he squeezed his hands on her butt and pushed her all the way down on him.

"That's how you like it, right?"

"Yes," she barely mumbled out as he proceeded to guide her up and down on him, increasing the speed with each passing moment. He had yet to actually move and she tensed at the thought.

"Look at me," he demanded through clinched teeth. "Just keep your eyes focused on me."

His piercing stare was sexy and commanding. Shuttering, the first wave of passion hit her out of nowhere and she clung to Broderick tightly while saying his name over and over. She buried her head in his shoulder but he lifted it up and caught her eyes with his.

"I want you to look at me. I want to see all of the different amorous expressions I'm producing on your beautiful face."

This time she couldn't answer as a moan rose from her throat and landed on his lips, which lingered on hers. She wanted to kiss him but the intensity of his stare alone caused sounds she couldn't comprehend to escape from her mouth so loud she was glad they were on a private island. He slowed down a tad, only to speed back up a moment later, but this time he met her gyrating hips with rising thrusts of his own. Tiffani tried her hardest to keep her eyes locked with his as she dug her nails into his shoulders. Tremors soared through her center as she clinched around him with no control of her own as their heat added to the heat of the blazing sun scorching her skin.

"Oh…my goodness, Broderick…it's so damn good."

"That's my girl. Look at you handling all of this." He popped her bottom.

She nodded in response. She was now completely

winded. He swept her up, laid her on her back and placed her legs over his shoulders. With one thrust, Broderick snuggled inside of her once more, shocking her body with exhilarating volts of satisfaction. Pinning her hands to the blanket, he gazed at her with a magnetic desire that made her elated to be a woman. Tiffani squeezed his hands for dear life as he began to unhurriedly stroke her, which caused her to tremor beneath him. Hoarse moans escaped her mouth. With each stroke he initiated, she felt herself following his command, and her hips began to fall in sync with his tempo.

Tiffani wanted to give all of herself to him. Her mind, body and heart needed to belong to him. Did he know that she'd never felt this strongly for a man before in such a short time? That he'd ignited a blaze in her and caused her to go weak all at the same time from just a simple smile or touch?

"I'm so glad you came with me," she croaked out.

"Me too, beautiful." He let go of her hands and placed his on both sides of her face. She then wrapped her arms around his neck and raised her head to kiss him with the same fervor as the movement of their hips.

Broderick's plunged deeper and faster, manifesting an orgasm that began in her center and rocketed through her body.

"Is it good, beautiful?" he asked in between their erratic kisses.

"Oh, yes. So…damn good."

"You're all mine, you hear me?"

"Yes, baby. All yours."

"You gonna climax with me, beautiful?" he asked as his thrusts became untamed and she felt him pulsing inside of her.

"Yes, Broderick! Please come."

Moments later, they had both climaxed and Tiffani lay sated, half on the blanket and half on the sand. Their lovemaking had scrunched the blanket under them. They cuddled in silence for a couple of minutes until Broderick started laughing.

"What's funny, babe?" she asked as her breathing almost returned to normal.

"Just look at us. We're covered in sweat and sand." He glided his fingers through her tangled hair. "You do not want to see your hair. We should probably go inside before a seagull passes by and mistakes it for her nest and lays an egg." He laughed uncontrollably.

"You're not funny." She sat up laughing as well and noticed they were indeed covered in sand. "Let's go rinse off under the outdoor shower and then I'll get dinner started. We have to eat that salmon and shrimp before we leave."

"I can't believe we only have one more night here. Perhaps next time we can bring KJ."

"That's a great idea. I think he'll love it here."

That night, after a candlelit dinner on the beach and an exquisite time of lovemaking in Broderick's bed, she lay wrapped in his comforting embrace. His head nestled in the crook of her neck as he snored peacefully. Every now and then he'd place a kiss to the back of her neck. Tiffani had never felt so serene and content with a man as she did with Broderick. Even though she never wanted to marry again, she couldn't imagine her life without him.

"Look at you all tanned and whatnot," Blythe sassed as she entered the bakery the Tuesday morning after Tiffani returned from the Florida Keys. "And what is that scarf around your neck trying to cover?" She joined Tiffani at the bistro table.

Closing her laptop, Tiffani groaned as she realized nothing ever got past her friend. "Let's just say I didn't go alone." She lightly touched the scarf that covered a few love bites she didn't want the world to see. She was too old for such things, plus she didn't want KJ questioning her again about the mosquito bites on her neck.

Blythe's eyes widened and her face lit up. "Oh my goodness! You're glowing."

"We had a wonderful time. I didn't even know he was coming until I woke up from a short nap on the plane and saw him sitting in front of me wearing a yummy smile."

"I'm so happy for you. Maybe I should find a man to *be* with in your sense of the term so it's not a real relationship. I kind of like that. No boundaries. Just be in the moment. And it seems to be working for you. I haven't seen you this bright eyed since we met, except when you cut the ribbon on the bakery."

"Yeah, Broderick is a really nice guy."

"Girl, I hear you. I just came by to tell you that I have a little information on the different groups who are vying for the shopping plaza."

"Let's go to my office." Tiffani grabbed her laptop from the table where she was updating her blog. "Mindy, I'll be back."

Once settled in her office, Tiffani poured some coffee and sat at her desk and Blythe plopped on the couch.

"Well, I don't know everything yet. But my source said this guy named Josh Powell who works for some big-time investor has been researching the property history and stats. There's several different groups but two are in the running and the one this Powell guy belongs to wants to tear down and start over."

"Any names?"

"Nope just Josh Powell's. The investors don't want their names known yet for whatever reason, but my source is still investigating. He said that one group has millions and they are willing to pay some astronomical price because they want to make this an eat, work and play type place like Atlantic Station in midtown."

"Wow. Do you know how much our leases would be? Out of this world." Tiffani opened her laptop and clicked on the blog post she had been working on.

"Girl, who you telling?" Blythe said, shaking her braided hair. "I've been sick to my stomach thinking about it. I just started making a steady profit last year."

"I barely made a profit this month, but business is really picking up. I'd hate to change locations."

Blythe rose from the couch. "I need to get going. I have a paint event in a few minutes with a bridal party. I just wanted you to know."

After she left, Tiffani read over her latest blog entry detailing her frustrations of big businesses swooping in and taking over small family-owned ones to make more millions. And although she actually liked the concept of the eat, work and play facility, she also knew the cost. She'd once considered a few of those locations but was unable to afford the lease.

"I don't know who you are, Josh Powell, or your millionaire friends, who think they can just take away people's livelihoods. You just better hope I never have the opportunity to meet you in person," she read out loud before pressing Publish.

Broderick sat at his desk at BJ Hollingsworth Corporation reading over the final contracts with Supreme Construction. It was one of the most lucrative investments he'd made in a long while and he was looking forward to reaping the benefits. Devin was building a small lakefront gated community with forty mansions. The floor plans started at two million and the properties surrounded a manmade lake. He was even considering buying one of the houses himself. His thoughts drifted to laying on the beach with Tiffani in his arms relaxing and discussing the world, politics or talking about absolutely nothing and simply enjoying each other while basking in the sun.

She was as close to perfect as possible. Running a successful bakery and raising her son without his father was commendable. She was beautiful on the inside and out and had to be the most loving person he'd ever met. He respected her so-called relationship concept but the more he was around her, he wanted her all to himself forever. That was going to be his next investment project.

Broderick opened his laptop and typed in the web address for her blog. He really wanted to call Tiffani, but he knew she was busy that day baking sweet potato pies for a large number of businesses having their annual Thanksgiving potluck dinners. He'd even placed an order for ten pies for his party later that week, much to Matilda's chagrin. To appease her, he'd told her she worked too hard and needed a break.

Clicking on the newest post, he saw that she'd just uploaded it an hour before. In it she discussed her ongoing frustrations with the shopping plaza possibly being sold and torn down within the next year, depending upon who bought it. He skimmed through it, as it seemed to be a rehashing of a conversation they'd had on the plane on the way home.

His heart contracted and stopped beating when he read the last sentence. He read it again hoping he was mistaken. Hoping that there were two Josh Powells in Atlanta with the same job. Tiny beads of perspiration formed on his forehead as he pushed away from his desk and stormed out of his office.

"Mr. Hollingsworth," Leslie called out frantically.

"Not now," he shouted louder than he ever had as he marched down the hall to Josh's office and flung the door open without knocking.

"Damn, man." Josh rose from his desk chair in utter shock and running a hand through his blond hair. "You scared me. What's wrong with you?"

Broderick stood in front of the desk and had to keep himself from yanking Josh by the tie. "What is the name of the shopping center in Dunwoody that Carl and Cedric told us about?"

"Premium Village."

Broderick banged his fists on the desk over and over. "Damn. Damn. Damn." He ran his hands over his head. "I don't believe this bullshit!"

"Calm down, man." Josh strode over to the wet bar and poured two glasses of bourbon. "What's wrong? Did someone already buy it?"

"No. I need you to call Cedric right now and take my name off the list of possible investors. We're out." He tried to calm down, but his pulse was racing.

Taken aback, Josh handed Broderick a glass. "Wait. What do you mean *we're out*?"

"Exactly what I just said." He breathed in and took a sip of the drink. The last thing he wanted was for Tiffani to find out that he was even considering buying the shopping center or, even worse, find out from someone other than him.

"Why all of sudden? I haven't even presented you with all of the facts yet."

"Just do it." The anger in him resurfaced as he turned to leave.

"Broderick, I know you just signed the contract with Devin, but I think you should still consider the shopping center, as well," Josh called after him.

Turning back around and stepping into his personal space, Broderick towered over Josh by at least five inches. "Maybe I didn't make myself clear," he began through clinched teeth. "Take my damn name off of the list right now."

"You're the boss," Josh said, holding up his hands in surrender.

Broderick backed away, mad at himself for shouting at his colleague. He'd been his trusted advisor and business manager since the very first investment and had never steered him in the wrong direction. But this wasn't business. It was personal this time. The woman he was falling in love with would be heartbroken if she thought he was involved.

"Call him now and come to my office immediately after."

Once settled back in his desk chair, he clicked on a picture of Tiffani on her website. Stirring around the drink in the glass, he sipped the rest and then threw the glass across the room. It shattered on the wall next to the door. A moment later, Leslie entered, saw the mess and shook her head.

"I'll clean up."

He stood and waved his hands in front of him. "No. No. I'll do it. Just cancel my appointments for today and call Samuel. Have him meet me out front in thirty minutes with the Bentley. I'm leaving for the day."

"Yes, sir," she said quietly with an empathetic expression before closing the door gently. But it soon opened again with Josh striding in.

"Well?" Broderick asked, placing his laptop in its case.

"I spoke to Cedric and told him we were no longer interested in investing with him in the shopping center. He asked about the restaurant chain. I told him he'd need to speak with you."

"Thank you. I'm not sure about the restaurant chain…um… I'm considering another option at the moment. For now, email me everything you found out about the Premium Village and the area. Also, if you have any financial information on the owner, I want that, too. If not, find out."

"Done." Josh walked over to Broderick. "Are you going to tell me what's up or leave me hanging?" he asked in a firm tone.

"I need to do something first and then we'll talk."

"Okay. I hope you know what you're doing," Josh said reluctantly.

"I hope so, too."

Chapter 10

"Hey, Broderick," Tiffani said as she answered the phone. She placed it between her ear and shoulder so she could use both hands to pour the sweet potato batter into the pie crust.

"Hey. How are you?"

"Better now that I'm hearing your voice." She couldn't believe the wide smile that had formed on her face. She hadn't spoken to him since he had called earlier just to say "good morning, beautiful." His voice in her ear always took her breath away.

"What's wrong?" he asked with concern.

"Just making pies. The last batch for now. And I saw the order you placed today."

"Cool. I wanted to talk to you about something. Are you free this evening?"

"Yes. KJ is staying with my parents tonight because I'll be here after closing filling a ton of orders for holiday parties and then I'll have to come back in the morning. What time were you thinking?"

"Doesn't matter. I really need to talk to you about something."

She frowned at his tone. Even though he was calm, she heard the same nervousness in his voice that KJ had when he was trouble. "Well, I'll be here."

After they hung up, she finished the pies and placed them in the oven. While cleaning up her mess, Kendall peeked her head into the kitchen.

"Hey, Blythe is here to see you."

"Tell her to come on through."

Blythe entered the kitchen, shaking her head with a solemn expression.

"What's wrong, hon?" Tiffani asked, setting the bowl down and walking toward her friend.

"Girl, you're sleeping with the enemy."

Tiffani sat on the bar stool icing cupcakes and waiting impatiently for Broderick to arrive. She'd been numb ever since Blythe had informed her that Broderick's name was associated with the investment group that wanted to tear down her business, among others. She was in utter shock and furious. Had he played her? Was he actually stopping by to see her, or was he really coming by the plaza to check it out? He'd bought desserts from her, painted at Blythe's place, bought lunch for them at the deli a few doors down and had even ordered the peonies for her from the florist on the other side. She wasn't aware if he'd visited other places there, but more than likely he had.

Frustrated, she slammed the icing bag on the counter after messing up two cupcakes in a row. Luckily, she always baked a couple of extra ones, but right now her hands were too shaky to continue. She chastised herself for falling for him and for even thinking that he would be someone she would even consider marrying. She'd fallen for his easy charm, his good looks, manly physique and that damn delicious smile he always bestowed upon her as if he were actually happy to see her.

Her cell phone vibrated in her apron pocket. She pulled it out to see a text message from Broderick stating that he was outside.

Breathing in, she headed toward the door. He was standing so eloquently yet authoritatively with a dashing smile that normally would melt her heart. Now she wanted to slap it off his face.

Unlocking the door, she opened it and moved back inside to let him in.

"Hey, beautiful." He leaned in to kiss her on the cheek but she stepped away from him to close and lock the door. A puzzled expression reached his features as he handed her a bag from The Cheesecake Factory. "I brought you dinner from your favorite restaurant."

She barely looked at him and he frowned as he set the bag on one of the bistro tables.

"It smells like sweet potatoes in here." Tilting his head, he swished his lips to the side. "What's wrong?"

She laughed sarcastically. "What's wrong? Where should I begin?" She grabbed a folder that was sitting on a bar stool and slammed it on his chest. "Seems like you, Mr. Hollingsworth, are trying to destroy what I'm trying to build." Her arms crossed over her chest as she waited for him to stop pretending he didn't know what the heck she was talking about.

His eyes glazed over the content in the folder as he shook his head. He reached out to her but she backed away.

"Don't touch me," she yelled. "How could you just lie to me this the entire time?"

"No, Tiffani, wait…it's not…"

"It's not what? What I think it is?" Her hand landed on her hip and she marched straight into his personal space and was practically eye level thanks to her wedge sandals. "I can read and it clearly states your name under the CBC Investors Group. I'm assuming the B is for Broderick, or in your case bastard." Pointing her finger on his chest, she stared coldly into his dark brown eyes. "A lying bastard!"

"Tiffani," he began in a calm tone. He then gently removed her finger from his chest and she instinctively took a step backward. "I didn't know that CBC was considering this plaza until earlier today when I read your blog post and saw Josh's name."

"Are you kidding me?" She ended up in his personal

space again. "How do you not know what you're going to invest in? It's your money."

"Because Josh is my business manager. He gathers all the details and presents everything to me at one time. Not in bits and pieces. Yes, I was aware that CBC was considering investing in a shopping plaza in Dekalb County, two actually, but I didn't know which ones. Do you know how many shopping plazas there are in this county? Hundreds. I told the other main partners, Cedric and Carl, that I really wasn't interested, but I'd have Josh do some research and I'd make a final decision if I liked the stats."

"How could you not inquire about names of the plazas that they presented to you?"

"When we discuss business they know to go to Josh with the details. They told me in a brief informal meeting about shopping centers and a restaurant chain I was more interested in."

She sauntered away from him and through the kitchen door with him on her heel. "I don't believe you."

He turned her softly around by the shoulders. "Sweetheart, I know you don't, but I don't have any reason to lie to you."

"You're a controlling arrogant ass at work. Your words. Not mine. Therefore, I'm sure you know everything that is going on with BJ Hollingsworth Corporation because it's your name and a brand that you built. Why wouldn't you want to know every detail up-front?"

"Tiffani," he said through clinched teeth, which

made her heart jump because she'd never seen him angry before. She wasn't going to let him scare her, though, so she didn't back off.

"I have investment ideas thrown at me every single damn day and not just from brick-and-mortar businesses. Everything from those stupid gadgets you see advertised on television to workout DVDs, music and other stuff, but it doesn't cross my desk because Josh and Leslie know not to present it to me until every fact is known. Therefore, Ms. Chase-Lake, I'm not aware of every minute detail until it's absolutely necessary. I just invested millions into Supreme Construction's upcoming project. That has been my main focus and you know this because we've discussed it."

Tiffani ran her hands down her face and breathed in deeply so the tears that desperately wanted to fall wouldn't.

"You started coming here right before I found out that Harvey was selling the place. Blythe's source stated Harvey had been meeting with different investment groups and individuals looking for the best deal months before he told the store owners. So cut the crap, Mr. Hollingsworth. You were only coming to check out the place."

He grabbed her to him and held her tight in his embrace. She tried to wiggle free, but he wouldn't budge. "I only came here to see you. That's it!"

"Not true. When we met, you stated your secretary would call and then you showed up. Clearly you wanted to check the place out." She continued to squirm, but it was no use as his strong muscular arms held her firmly in place.

"I was coming to check *you* out."

"Liar. And to think I let you meet my son… He likes you a lot."

He rested his forehead on hers and inhaled. "I'm not lying to you." His voice was barely above a whisper.

"Get out," she demanded, pointing toward the door.

"Don't do this, Tiffani."

"You got what you wanted, right? You had sex with the cupcake girl and now pretty soon you'll own the place. I'll have to find a new home for Sweet Treats because I won't be able to afford the new lease."

"No, no I won't. I told Josh to take my name off of the list of investors for the plaza. I don't know what will happen, but I'm no longer a part of it. I remembered how hurt you were the day you found out that Harvey was selling and you we're right… If the group I belonged to wins the bid, they're tearing it down, buying the acres behind it that are for sale and making this a work, live and play place. I saw the preliminary plans today. Yes, the lease is much higher than what you're paying now."

"Can they still buy it without you?"

"Oh, yeah. There were five of us, but the money that goes in isn't just to buy the plaza. That's just the tip of the iceberg. It's for the expansion. We're talking tens of millions overall. The investors, and not just CBC, want the property because of the location."

"Mmm…well. Thank you for that tidbit of information," she said sarcastically, wrestling herself loose from his embrace. If he thought everything was cool now, he was sadly mistaken. Leaning against the counter for support, she breathed in as her next words weighed heavily on her tongue and her heart. "Now if you would just leave."

"Tiffani…" He stepped toward her.

"Stop," she demanded, holding up her hand.

Grabbing her hand, he held it against his heart. "I just told you the truth."

She snatched it away and gave him an icy stare. "Please leave."

"If that's what you want."

Dropping her hand, Broderick trekked to the kitchen door as she stood in the same spot, frozen. She sighed hard as his hand twisted the doorknob, and she prayed he'd hurry the hell up. However, he glanced over his shoulder, raked his gaze over her and held her eyes in a gripping trance with his. She stifled a gulp as her heart palpitated at an overzealous pace. She couldn't believe the man she thought she was falling in love with had betrayed her.

"This isn't over, beautiful."

Tiffani held her breath until she heard the bell on the door. She waited a few more minutes before going out front to lock the door and set the alarm. That's when the tears fell and she rushed back to her office to let it all out.

* * *

Broderick strummed his fingers on the steering wheel as he contemplated his decision to finally visit his father after five years. The last time had ended in a huge argument over money. Now, besides an occasional phone call, the two barely spoke. He breathed in deeply and thought about Tiffani. She was the one who had suggested he visit his father and now that he was actually going, they were no longer together. It had been a few days since their breakup. He'd tried calling, texting and dropping by the bakery, but she refused to see him or talk to him. He understood she was hurting and it hurt him, as well. The pain and betrayal on her face had been caused by him. And although he honestly hadn't known Premium Village was one of the shopping centers the investment group was considering, it still had wedged a sword between them, and he hated it.

Broderick had finally found a woman he could confide in, trust and be in a committed, monogamous relationship with. He'd dated and had girlfriends, but he wasn't dating them for long-term reasons and had never felt a true connection with any of them. He wasn't a millionaire playboy like a lot of his colleagues who'd identified themselves as players or bachelors for life. He'd always wanted to get married and have children. But he simply hadn't found the one woman he could envision doing so with, until he'd laid eyes on Tiffani. She was loving, considerate, and sweet and had a good heart. He loved the fact that she was a hardworking, single mother with her own business. He knew it had hurt her when she'd found out that plaza was being sold, and he knew it had to have hurt worse when she found out his name was on the list of possible investors who would steal her livelihood and independence away.

When she'd told him about the "be in the moment" type of relationship, he went along with it because he figured he'd be able to convince her otherwise. His plan had seemed to work, but now she hated him. That didn't mean he was giving up. He'd fallen for her. Hell, he'd fallen for the kid, too. Broderick couldn't imagine his life without them and was determined to win Tiffani back and convince her they belonged together. Being without her made him realize just how much he loved her, and he knew in his heart she loved him, too. He had some things in the works and truly hoped it would prove to her he'd had her best interest in mind all along.

As he pulled up to the retirement community, it dawned him that he was about to see his father, Roderick Hollingsworth. Since he hadn't been in his life like a real father, he'd given him the nickname, Rod. Broderick could not imagine forming his lips to call him father or dad. He didn't feel Rod was befitting of the title. Broderick parked his Bentley in the space next to the black Lexus GS300 he'd bought for his father a few years ago. He'd hoped it would've been a peace offering but instead Rod had questioned why it wasn't a Bentley.

Broderick turned the car off but didn't get out. He wasn't sure if he was making the best decision. It had seemed right when Tiffani had made the suggestion, but now he wasn't so sure. He already wasn't in the best mood because of his estranged relationship with Tiffani. The last thing he wanted to do was argue with his father. He glanced at his cell phone on the passenger seat. He needed to talk to her. He needed to hear her tell him to man up and he'd be fine. But he knew she wouldn't answer his call or any text messages. He decided to call anyway and if she didn't answer, he'd leave a voice mail so at least she would know he'd taken her advice and visited his father.

He breathed in and pushed her number on the screen. She answered on the fifth ring.

"Yes?" she asked in a curt tone.

She's clearly still mad. "Hi, there," he said in an upbeat manner. "I just wanted to tell you that I'm sitting outside my father's place. I'm about to go in. I think." Sighing, he ran his hand down his face.

"You think? You drove way out there and now you're not going to go in?"

"I just don't want to argue."

"Well, if you go in with that mentality then you will. Think positive. Does he know you're coming?"

He smiled at her pep talk. Even though Tiffani was clearly upset with him from the way she'd answered the phone, she'd pushed aside her hurt to encourage him. That was one of the reasons he loved her. The love she had within her was unconditional.

"Yeah, I called him yesterday about visiting him today. It's his birthday."

"So be a man and go in. Did you dress down?"

"Yes. A sweater and some khakis, like you suggested when we were on the island."

He heard her breath intake when he mentioned the island, and thoughts of lying with her naked, sexy body in his embrace filled his head. Perhaps the same thoughts clouded her thoughts at that very moment because she was silent before speaking again.

"Get off the phone with me and go inside."

"I'm glad you answered."

"I almost didn't. Honestly, I was only answering to tell you to stop calling me."

"Oh, so I guess you don't want to know how it goes."

She groaned. "I do because I'm glad you decided to go, but maybe you should just send me a short text. I promise I'll read it."

"Okay. Thank you, Tiffani.

"Take care, Broderick." She hung up before he could say goodbye.

He gazed at the screen as it went back to her contact information. He then perused a picture of her when they were on the island. They'd just finished making love not too long before, and he'd snapped the picture as she sat on an Adirondack chair on the beach wearing one of his dress shirts. Her hair hung over her left shoulder in a messy array of curls and she was smiling as if blissful. He'd hoped he was the reason for her glowing face and had snapped the picture unbeknownst to her.

Still staring at the picture, Broderick's heart tensed as he thought of the last time he'd seen her face. He had evoked a different emotion from her that day, and even though he didn't have an actual picture of it, her expression was mentally etched in his brain. Exhaling, he turned off the phone and grabbed the gift bag on the passenger seat.

Once he made it to the entrance of the town house, he inhaled and rung the doorbell. Moments later, his father opened the door and it was like looking into a mirror. His father was the same height and build and had dark butterscotch skin and the same haircut and beard. The only difference was Rod's hair was all gray, but at sixty-six he was still in shape and overall his general health was fine.

"Hello, twin," Rod said in a voice just as deep as his.

"Happy birthday, Rod." Broderick handed him the gift bag and stepped inside the foyer.

"Thank you. Let's go up to the living room and have a seat. I made some chicken and baked potatoes with a salad if you're hungry."

"That sounds great."

After they were settled with their food and beer in the eat-in kitchen area, Broderick felt a little better about his decision to visit Rod. Rod caught him up on his life and Broderick was truly impressed by his accomplishments. Thanks to the rehab facility on the property, Rod no longer did drugs and even though he was drinking a beer with him now, he rarely drank alcohol either. He spent his days helping the maintenance crew with the grounds, planting shrubbery and flowers to keep active.

"So can I open my gift now?" Rod asked, nodding toward the bag sitting on the table.

Broderick bobbed his head as he chewed his chicken. "Go ahead. This chicken is good, by the way."

"Thanks." Rod drew the bag toward him and stood as he flung the tissue paper out. "A little honey who lives here taught me how to season it just right."

"Mmm-hmm. I bet."

"Well, you know. You aren't the only one who gets the girls. I've seen you in pictures at social events around Atlanta. Chip off the old block."

Broderick wanted to protest Rod's last statement, because besides looks, he was nothing like his father. However, he remembered what Tiffani said about being positive and making amends, so he took a swallow of his beer instead.

"Ah, man," Rod exclaimed, taking the tablet box out of the bag. "This is out of sight. I've been wanting one of these. I don't always feel like being bothered by the computer and my cell phone screen is too small when I'm searching the net."

"Glad you like it. There's one more box in the bag."

Rod dug around and pulled out the cell phone box.

"Perfect. I needed a new cell phone."

"Great. I'm glad you like it. It's actually already activated along with the tablet, and both monthly costs are still on me. You'll just need to download your data from your other cell phone to the new one. It's the same number."

"Wow, this is wonderful. Thanks, son." Rod held out his hand to shake Broderick's, but instead he rose and gave his father a hug.

Rod squeezed tighter. "Now this is the best gift. A hug from my son. Thank you."

Broderick closed his eyes and hugged his father tighter. "You're welcome, Dad." He cleared his throat and released him. "Now let's eat before this food gets cold."

After they ate, they retreated to the living room to watch basketball and to continue catching up.

"So you seeing someone steady?"

Broderick sighed and sipped his beer. He'd been having a great time and for a moment had forgotten about his current situation with Tiffani.

Rod scratched his beard. "Oh, I see. There is someone but things aren't going too hot at the moment?"

"Something like that. It's complicated. She's mad at me for something she thought I did but I didn't. Even after I told her the truth she still doesn't believe me."

"Well, maybe she's not the right woman for you. Is she one of those gold-digging chicks after your millions?"

"No. I don't even think she cares about my money.

She has her own business. She's not a millionaire, but with hard work and more exposure, she could very well be."

"So what's special about her? Why did your face nearly crumble when I asked?"

"Because Tiffani is the one. She reminds me of my mother, loving and warm, with a big heart."

"Tiffani. That's a pretty name. You have a picture?"

Broderick took his cell phone and scrolled until he found a picture of Tiffani when they were having lunch on Key West. Her radiant smile and rosy cheeks made her even more adorable. His chest tightened at the thought of never having her sweet smile bestowed on him again.

"Beautiful girl. They're usually the high maintenance ones, too." Rod chuckled and handed back the cell phone.

Broderick glanced at her picture once more before closing it. "Nope, not her. Her main concern is her son and her bakery, but yes she is beautiful. Inside and out."

"Mmm…you know I messed up with your mother. She was a lovely woman, but then we got hooked on drugs. Our relationship was never the same after that. I regret moving away and leaving you two. She had a fiery temper and after she kicked me out and divorced me, I spiraled downhill for many years."

"Yeah, so did she. I wish she was still here. She's the only person that has ever shown me love."

"I've always loved you, son, even though I know you think I don't."

Broderick chuckled sarcastically. "Well, you had an odd way of showing it." As soon as he said it, he felt bad. He was supposed to avoid the usual conversation that set up their usual argument. The one where he'd call his father ungrateful and his father would in turn tell him that he should've tried harder to save his mother.

Rod sipped his beer and pondered for a moment, nodding his head with a pursed lip. "I know I said some pretty rough things to you over the years but that was the drugs talking. Besides, you proved me wrong. You're a very successful young man and I'm proud of you. You own almost half of Atlanta. Heck, don't you own this retirement community?"

Broderick was stunned with where the conversation had drifted. Maybe his father was turning over a new leaf. He'd never told him he was proud of him. Ever.

"I used to. I sold my shares, but I still make sure they take care of you as if I do."

"I appreciate that, Broderick. I'm very proud of you and your accomplishments. You didn't let your environment define you or the fact that I wasn't supportive. You made it out of the 'hood. Even though I'm sure you still have your street smarts. I doubt you've let anyone get over on you in the corporate world."

"You know me well because most of the deals I've made I didn't use anything I learned out of a textbook. Except how to remain professional."

"That's my boy." Rod reached out and gave Broderick a high five.

"Thank you. So we'll take this one step at a time?"

"How about two? I ain't getting any younger." The men shared a laugh and toasted their beer bottles.

"Um…what are you doing for Thanksgiving next week?" Broderick asked. It was out of the blue, but considering his original dinner plans had probably been cancelled by Tiffani, he figured he'd spend it with his father.

"Well, actually you know the little honey I was telling you about?" A wicked smile formed across Rod's face. "We're going to the north Georgia Mountains for some cabin fun."

Broderick almost spit his beer out at the thought. Knowing his father was still having sex was too much information. "Cool. Is she younger than you?" Broderick asked.

"Yep, fifty-nine and just as sassy and feisty as she wants to be. Her name is Dottie and we met in the gym, but I'm game for Christmas if you are."

"Christmas would be perfect. You and Dottie can come stay with me for a few days." *In the guest room on another wing of the mansion so I won't hear your cabin fun.*

"That sounds great. Haven't been to your place in awhile. I saw in a local architectural magazine where the wife of the US Senator…what's his name… Monroe, yeah, his wife did a great job on redecorating your home."

"Yes, Megan Monroe. Actually her cousin is who I'm dating…well, I was dating. I don't know."

"You'll get her back, man. You're a Hollingsworth. Who can resist our charm and good looks?"

"You're funny. You know, she's the reason I'm here. She told me it was time to come see you, and I couldn't agree more. Maybe that's why she was in my life—to bring me back to you."

"That's a wonderful analogy, son, but I think you're in love with this woman. Give her some time. Women have to have a cooling-off period because right now she's still hot. Catch her when she's simmered down some."

Broderick soaked in his father's advice. She may have simmered down a tad considering she finally answered the phone when he'd called and encouraged him to get out of the car. He decided to put a peg in it for now.

"Dad, let's go shoot some pool over at the rec center."

"That sounds like a plan. I'll go grab my coat."

Broderick was elated that things were going well with his father, who he now felt the urge to call "Dad." Now, if he could get the love of his life back all would be well in his world. As his father had said, he was a Hollingsworth man, and he was determined to win his woman back.

Chapter 11

"Hey, Tiffani!" Sasha Monroe exclaimed as she stood to hug her. "Great to see you."

"Same here." Tiffani smiled and turned her attention to her twin cousins, who were sitting together in the restaurant's booth. She had to do a double take because both of them had their hair in buns on the top of their heads. Even though they were identical, she almost always knew who was who. However, she'd been in such a daze the past week from lack of sleep due to a load of orders and from her breakup with Broderick. Even though she kept trying to convince herself it wasn't an actual breakup because they weren't ever in a real relationship, it sure did hurt the same way. But she was glad that she'd gotten herself out early before she fell for him even more. She'd been closer to the edge than she realized, and she needed to save herself before falling completely over.

She slid into the booth next to Sasha, Megan and Sydney's cousin-in-law, and looked at the twins once again, this time recognizing who was who. Sydney, a criminal profiler for the Georgia Bureau of Investigations, was seated across from her and eyed her peculiarly. Tiffani had a hunch that her cousin was trying to figure out what was wrong without asking.

"What, Syd?" Tiffani inquired, perusing The Cheesecake Factory menu even though she already knew what she was going to order. She was famished because she hadn't eaten much lately; even though it was only lunchtime, she wanted the dinner version of fish and chips with a salad.

Syd shrugged and glanced at her own menu before placing her eyes on Tiffani again. "Nothing, except that your body language is screaming at me."

Tiffani chuckled and played with the ring on her right hand. "Girl, my body is screaming at me. My muscles are sore, and I haven't slept in days. I'm grateful for the business, but because Thanksgiving's coming up, I've had extra orders for cupcakes for schools in the area. I'm also baking pies and assembling dessert platters for businesses having office parties leading up to the holiday. Luckily, Mindy is assisting me. She's a really good protégé."

Tiffani was reminded of the brief conversation she'd

had with Broderick's secretary, Leslie, that morning confirming the pickup time for the ten pies for their company party. Tiffani had caught a snippet of Broderick's deep, powerful voice in the background asking Leslie for something. He'd sent roses to the bakery the day before, but he hadn't contacted her since he'd visited his father other than a short text message to say they were taking it one day at a time. She was honestly happy for them.

Syd nodded her head and swished her lips to the side with smack. "Yeah, well I was referring to the lack of sleep caused by your breakup with Broderick."

"It wasn't a breakup. You have to be in a relationship in order to have an actual breakup. We just aren't seeing each other anymore because he's a lying dog."

Megan leaned over and placed her hand on Tiffani's. "But what if he's not lying? I've known and worked with Broderick for many years and while he's in the know of his company, he's not a micromanager. He has a trusted team of advisors."

"It doesn't matter. I needed to get out before I got too attached. For a moment, I'd gotten caught up and I actually was having fantasies of spending the rest of my life with him. I could actually see us frolicking on the beach, playing with KJ and being a family. I think it's best I stopped seeing him when I did." She heard herself saying it and her heart cracked a little.

"Sweetie, are you just trying to find a way out of the relationship because you've fallen for him harder than you wanted to?" Megan quizzed. Even though her twin was the profiler, she knew Tiffani very well because of their similar personalities.

"No… I don't know. Maybe. I just keep thinking about my marriage with Keith and how unhappy I was. Now I feel like me again. I don't have to worry about being belittled or called out my name by a man who didn't appreciate his wife. I just don't want to take that risk, which is why I created the 'be in the moment' relationship. But I ended up falling for the man anyway."

Megan gave her a half smile. "I understand. I really do. I was hesitant about dating Steven because of my ex cheating on me. Steven was labeled as the playboy politician, but I had to look beyond that and grasp that he loved me and was nothing like my ex. It took me a minute, but I was glad it wasn't too late when I realized it. You'll have your aha moment if it's meant to be."

Sighing, Tiffani closed her menu and sipped her water, hoping it would cool down the warmth that arose whenever she thought about Broderick. She was thankful when the waiter stopped by to take their orders. As they waited for their meals, she was able to change the subject by asking Sasha about her upcoming nuptials. Even though it was about a subject she really didn't want to discuss, it was all her cousin-in-law spoke about lately. Tiffani didn't mind as long as it kept her mind off of Broderick.

Sasha's warm brown face beamed with delight as she ran her fingers through her pixie cut. "Well, everything is pretty much set for June. Devin and I are excited. Since I'm the VP of marketing for Pinnacle Hotels, I've received a great discount on the ballroom and a honeymoon suite. I'm delighted that you're going to make our wedding cakes, Tiffani. I loved the cakes at Syd's wedding. Devin told me to tell you he wants his groom's cake shaped like a Ferris wheel for sentimental reasons." Sasha released another radiant smile as she always did when she mentioned Devin's name.

"That's a great idea. I'll start practicing," Tiffani replied. "Were you able to secure an appointment with Elle Lauren?"

"Mother and I are flying to New York to meet with her this weekend. I can't believe you all are friends with Elle Lauren and she's designing the dresses for the bridal party and me. I'm overjoyed she's squeezing me in because of you guys." Sasha paused for a moment as if she wasn't sure if she wanted to continue. "Do you think Braxton would mind if I invited her to the wedding?"

Tiffani cringed on Elle's behalf at the thought. "Mmm…you can invite her but she probably won't come. We all invited her to our weddings and she politely declined. Not sure how Braxton would feel. They were together ages ago but he was a no-show to their wedding and it broke her heart. She was very much in love with him while he was very much in love with his music."

Sydney chimed in. "When I went to my last gown

fitting, Braxton called to verify a song for my wedding. Elle's face cracked in a thousand pieces when I pressed the speaker by mistake while slipping my T-shirt on. It took her a minute to regroup, so I could only imagine what would happen if she saw him in person. He doesn't discuss her much, but when he saw my dress, he said, 'It's beautiful but everything she does is beautiful.' So feel free to invite her, but she'll decline."

Sasha sipped her wine and nodded her head. "You never know. After Devin and I broke up the day after graduation, I never wanted to see or hear from him ever again. However, when he walked through my door last Christmas, every single emotion I had for him rushed back and I knew I wanted to spend the rest of my life with that man. I never stopped loving him. It was fate and faith that brought us back together. We're soul mates, just like Bryce and Sydney. Who knew that two people who always argued back and forth would end up together?"

Sydney nodded with a wide smile. "I have to agree, Sasha. We still argue but only because it leads to the bedroom." She winked and all of the ladies laughed.

"Are you and Devin coming for Thanksgiving dinner?" Megan asked Sasha.

"No, we're going to Savannah to visit my parents."

"Why do I keep forgetting Thanksgiving is next week?" Sydney asked.

"Because you're a newlywed," Megan answered. "You're too busy riding motorcycles with Bryce."

"So true. I sure do love that man," Syd said with a saucy grin.

Once their food arrived, Tiffani tuned out the conversation as it continued with Thanksgiving, wedding talk and marriage in general. With her recent hectic schedule, she'd forgotten about the Thanksgiving dinner at her home next week. Luckily, everyone was bringing a dish to go with the turkey and ham she was baking. Normally she didn't bake a ham, but Broderick had asked for one because it was his favorite. She'd wanted him to have a nice Thanksgiving dinner with her family because he hadn't had one in years. Her heart ached a little now that he wouldn't be coming, but she brushed it off, remembering he was trying to steal her livelihood and independence away from her. She still couldn't believe she hadn't seen right through him. She chastised herself for not realizing he could be one of the potential buyers of the plaza because, after all, he was a freaking real estate developer and investor. The only reason she didn't consider him was because, according to an article she'd read, his focus was on properties such as hotels, casinos and high-end condos and lofts.

Tiffani knew the emotions she had for Broderick were real. Deep down a part of her sensed he'd been telling the truth about not knowing the name of the plaza his investment group was considering. She thought about what Megan and Sasha had said about finding their way to love. Tiffani wasn't sure what the future held for her, but warding off falling in love again was the only way she could see to protect her heart. However, her heart was hurting worse than it ever had and she missed Broderick more than she cared to admit.

Tiffani checked the Roman numeral clock on the wall next to the menu board as she and Kendall brought out the ten sweet potato pies for Leslie to pick up. She'd said between three and four and it was a few minutes to three. Setting the last one in a box on the back counter, she tended to a customer who had a question about her vegan cupcakes. Out of the corner of her eye, she spotted a black Bentley pull up and park on the curb next to the bakery. Her heart skipped, but she brushed off her fear. He wouldn't possibly come pick up the pies. That wasn't in his job description, but then again neither had been ordering cupcakes for his event way back when. His driver emerged, and she figured he was coming inside the bakery. Instead, he went to the back door and Tiffani's breath became wedged in her throat.

There he was, as suave and handsome as always. His brown suit hung on his masculine body as if he'd just stepped off the runway. Broderick flashed a pleasant smile to someone on the sidewalk before entering her store and resting his gaze on her. He glanced at the bistro tables and raised a cocky eyebrow as he apparently realized that she'd made flower arrangements for each table with the yellow and pink roses he'd sent.

He waited in line behind the customer Tiffani was speaking with, and her heart fluttered uncontrollably.

He was the last person she expected to see stroll in and he had the audacity to exude his debonair and refined persona. For some odd reason he appeared extra sexy and mouthwatering, and she had to remind herself that she was supposed to be upset with him. Even though all she wanted to do was fling herself over the counter like a martial artist and kiss him. Once the customer left, he stepped up to the counter and handed Tiffani the order receipt.

"I have an order for ten sweet potato pies, beautiful." He cracked a sexy smile. "Are they ready?"

"Yes, they're all packed and ready to go in the box behind me." She grabbed the box and set them in front of him. "You're free to go. Leslie paid for them already."

A sly smirk crossed his features. "They sure do smell great. One of my favorite desserts. I love sweet things to eat." Pausing, he leaned in closer to her and whispered, "But of course you know that first hand." He lifted the box off of the counter. "Have a great day, sweetheart."

Once he left, she exhaled and glanced over to see Kendall staring with a wide grin. "You have two men after you. Here comes Nixon Brown now." She nodded toward the door as Nixon walked in with a bright smile and beelined straight to Tiffani.

Tiffani groaned in her head while wearing the loveliest expression she could muster. It was bad enough Broderick had just left her with a visual of his head between her thighs, but now entered Nixon, a regular customer who always flirted with her. He was harmless, though, and she usually didn't mind. But today she wasn't in the mood.

"Hey, Tiffani. You have any of my favorite coffee crumb cakes left?" Nixon asked, perusing the display case.

"We sure do. I was wondering where you were this morning. It's nearly three o'clock."

"Doctor's appointment." He pointed his finger on the glass. "And two of those macaroons."

As she placed his items in a small box, the ringing of the bell tore her eyes to the door to see Broderick enter once again. "Excuse me, Mr. Brown," she said before directing her attention toward Broderick. "Is there something wrong with your order, Mr. Hollingsworth?" she asked, concerned. She'd made sure to count the pies while placing them in the box.

His expression hinted he hated her calling him Mr. Hollingsworth. "No, the order is fine. I have a meeting on this side of town soon and since you offer free Wi-Fi with a purchase, I've decided to stay and get some work done on my laptop."

He patted the computer bag she hadn't realized he was carrying and goose bumps prickled her skin. Of course, she couldn't kick him out, but she could ignore or rather annoy him to the point where he'd want to leave.

"Certainly, Mr. Hollingsworth. That table over there has a plug. If you need anything, ask Kendall."

Broderick nodded as a thank you and retreated to

the table. He took off his suit coat and flung it on the back of the chair. His dress shirt did nothing to hide his strong muscles, and for a moment she lost her train of thought as she recalled all the ways his biceps and chest had flexed when they'd made love.

She snapped back to her customer. "I'm sorry about that, Nixon. Was there anything else you wanted?" Tiffani made sure to ask in the sweetest voice ever.

He chuckled and scanned the display case again. "Nope, not unless the pretty baker will finally go out with me."

She giggled. "You always flatter me."

She watched Broderick as his eyebrow raised. His eyes were on the laptop screen, but she knew his ears were on her conversation with Nixon.

"Just speaking the truth, but it doesn't hurt to ask, Ms. Lady." He handed her his debit card. "I'm sure you get asked out all the time by customers."

"Mmm…sometimes. I'd say Kendall more than me. She's young and in college."

"Well, her boss has it going on. But as lovely as you are, I'm sure you have a man."

"Nope. Just me, myself and I. I'm *very* single. Just not ready to date at this moment. I thought I was, but some men just can't be trusted." She glanced over and noticed Broderick twist his lips to the side.

"Well, you know I'm interested if you ever want to go out." Grabbing her hand when she returned the card, he kissed her knuckle. "Ciao, bella." He winked and strode out with his desserts.

"Corny bastard," Broderick mumbled under his breath as he rapidly typed. "Ciao, bella? Really?"

"He's not so bad. Maybe I should go out with him." She shrugged and walked into the kitchen so she could exhale. Broderick's presence and cologne was wreaking havoc on her. When the kitchen door opened, she expected to see Kendall or Mindy, not Broderick standing there like a bull ready to knock over the matador.

"What are you doing back here?"

"We need to talk."

His voice had deepened, and she thought she saw steam rising from his head. She couldn't believe he was actually jealous over a harmless conversation with Nixon.

"We don't have anything to talk about," she said, trying to walk past him. But Broderick dragged her by the waist to him and crashed his lips hard on her quivering ones, muffling the protests she tried to make. He stumbled them into her office and then closed the door with his shoe.

Backing Tiffani against the door, he showed no mercy as his hands roamed under the hem of her sweater. The warmth of his palms on her skin was pure torture as tingles tore through her. She hated that her lips and body were responding to him this way. Her thoughts screamed to push him away, but her heart loved the way he kissed her in an untamed, invigorating rhythm that her tongue eagerly responded to in the same fashion. She glided her hands to his beard and pulled him deeper into her as their pace increased.

She wanted to stop him, but she couldn't. Her heart and body were under a spell that he'd cast and she couldn't break. The sound of his zipper broke a gasp from her and he trailed his tongue to her neck while he wrestled with the button on her pants. He tugged them down along with her panties as she kicked off her shoes. Kneeling down to the floor, he raised her right leg over his shoulder and dove straight into her center. Thanks to the mere touch of his hot tongue, a moan flew out of her mouth as she held on to his head to balance herself. Shudders ripped through her body as he continued to stimulate her more and more with his wicked tongue dance that circled between her folds. Tiffani didn't know how much more she could handle as she felt an orgasm on the rise.

Broderick worked his way back up to her neck as he reached around to his back pocket and pulled out his wallet. She licked her tongue over her lips as she saw him retrieve a condom. She shook with anticipation as he put it on.

"You actually had a condom in your wallet?"

"I have to be prepared around you," he said, lifting her up by the bottom, She circled her legs around his waist as he plunged into her all at once. "I want you all the time."

"Oh… Broderick. Mmm…" Clutching his shoulders,

she gave up trying to talk because she knew the words would sound like nonsense. Instead, she buried her head in his chest to muffle her incoherent moans. After all, she was in her office and not on a secluded island.

He carried her to the small couch as he continued thrusting in and out of her quickly. His intense stare as he laid her down was the onset of the first shudder that was lit like a bomb and ready to explode. He buried himself even deeper and she let out a pent-up moan. She couldn't help it. The man knew how to stroke her to evoke whatever it was he wanted her to do.

"That's how you want it, beautiful?" he asked gruffly.

"Yes."

"I bet that corny dude couldn't make you feel like this, could he?" He pumped harder and she wrapped her arms around his neck to hold on from the force.

"No," she answered breathlessly.

"Who's making you feel like this?"

"You."

"Who? I need you to look at me and say my name." He placed his forehead on hers and spread her legs wider.

"Broderick… Jerold Hollingsworth…" she panted out as they fell off the couch and onto the floor, but he never let her go as he continued to stroke in and out of her. The hot kisses he placed on her neck and the intensity of their lovemaking shattered her orgasm through her. She buried her head in his chest to deaden the sounds she so desperately needed to make.

Broderick pulled out of her and repositioned them so that she was on all fours. She placed her hands on the couch and cooled her panting down as he stood and slipped out of his pants. He then slid his body over hers and placed his blazing tongue on the back of her neck, which released a cry from her that she buried in the cushion. He moved his hand around to her breasts, kneading and massaging them. She banged her fists on the couch, and she wasn't sure how much more stimulation she could handle. Tiffani was so immersed with his tongue and hands on her body that a surprising wail escaped her when he entered with one long thrust.

He held on to her hips tightly and slowly pulled her all the way out from him and then all the way back with one long motion, over and over, speeding up every time. Tiffani couldn't control her fervent moans that increased with every second. She hoped no one could hear her next door or in her own place of business, for that matter.

He leaned over and whispered in her ear with a naughty chuckle, "I'm only moving your hips. I haven't even begun yet." He turned her face around, licked his tongue toward her mouth and kissed her with so much urgency and desire that she honestly didn't know if she could handle anything else. And then he began to thrust into her so powerfully and deep her orgasms began to overlap each other, sending her into oblivion.

"You coming for me, baby?" he inquired with his lips on her as he slapped her bottom.

"Oh, yes. Please don't stop."

The raw, wild pleasure and pain seemed as if it would never end and knowing Broderick's endurance, it would be a while. But she didn't want it to end. She'd craved and missed him the past few days and all of her repressed feelings for him were coming out as she climaxed. Clutching him, she felt him pulsating inside of her as he slammed into her and vibrated behind her with a long, screeching howl.

Broderick leaned over and kissed the few tears that had rolled down her cheeks and gathered her in his arms on the couch. Kissing her forehead, he rubbed her sore bottom where he had slapped it a few times.

She settled her eyes on his. "This doesn't mean I'm no longer upset with you."

He chuckled. "I know, but I told you this isn't over yet."

"Mmm...perhaps. But *this* doesn't mean I don't want to go out with the corny dude," she teased.

"Trust me, after the way I just made love to your mind, you'll never want nor need another man to touch you *ever* again." Releasing her from his embrace, he picked up his pants from the floor and stepped into the bathroom.

Broderick's words replayed in her head, and she groaned silently because she knew he was telling the truth. After that escapade, she couldn't fathom any other man in her life. He came out moments later, and she still sat satisfied on the couch.

"I need to leave. I really do have a meeting at Seasons 52 in about thirty minutes. Thanks for the sweet potato pies." He winked and walked out the door.

After freshening up, Tiffani strolled out of her office ten minutes later hoping for dear life that no one in the shop had heard them. Braxton's latest jazz CD always played in the background at a low enough volume for people to converse but loud enough to drown out whatever noise came from the kitchen. And because her office was in the back of the kitchen maybe no one had heard her fanatical cries.

She stepped out and spotted Kendall at the cash register ringing up customers and Mindy placing some cupcakes in a to-go box. However, when she saw Blythe sitting on the window seat reading a romance novel and pursing her lips, she knew it was going to be a downhill conversation.

"Hey, girl."

Blythe stood, placed the Brenda Jackson novel back on the shelf and took Tiffani by the hand. "Let's step into my office for a chat."

"Oh…okay, or we can go back to mine."

"No, not right now. I don't want to sit anywhere in *your* office."

Tiffani gulped and looked around as Blythe pulled her out the door.

Once they made it to Blythe's brightly orange-painted office in the back of her studio, she pulled out two wineglasses from a cabinet, opened a bottle of white zinfandel and poured some into each glass. She handed one to Tiffani and sat next to her on the couch.

"I'm sure you could use this right about now."

"Its four o'clock in the afternoon," Tiffani said, taking a sip.

"Yep, but it's five o'clock somewhere and after what I just heard, you probably need something stronger. Heck, I need something stronger."

Tiffani laughed so hard she snorted. "Girl… I don't know what to say."

"You said plenty not too long ago. Chile, my paint session had just ended and I was cleaning up when all of a sudden I hear a man's deep, commanding voice and a screeching woman on the other side of the wall."

"I wasn't screeching."

"Lies. Yes, you were. My assistant called me up front, and I glanced out the window to see a black Bentley parked on the curb."

"No comment."

Tilting her head, a concerned expression graced Blythe's face and she patted Tiffani's hand. "Are you back together or was it one of those breakup sex episodes?"

"You have to be in a relationship to break up. But no, we're not back together, even though he wants to be, and I know what I said didn't make any sense considering we weren't in an actual relationship." She set the wine down on the coffee table and leaned her head back on the couch.

"As long as it makes sense to you. I just know you've been moping around for the past week and now you're glowing. He's pulled out of the investment group so maybe there was some truth to what he said. The shortage of good, honest men is real. Don't let him go because of miscommunication or lack of knowledge."

Tiffani stood and stretched her sore body as the alarm sounded on her cell phone. It was time to leave to pick up KJ from his after-school tutorial session.

"Yeah, we'll see. Thanks for the advice." As she walked out, her mind was in a frenzy. She cared for Broderick a lot. No, she knew that was a big lie. She'd fallen in love with him, but she was scared of losing herself in another relationship, even though she couldn't see herself without him.

Later on that night as she was drifting off to sleep, her cell phone beeped. Retrieving it from the night-stand, she squinted and saw a text message from Broderick.

Call me if you're still up.

Why?

Because I want to hear your sweet, raspy voice in my ear.

Go to bed, old man.

I'm leaving in the morning for a trip to Arkansas. Some business associates I know want to open up a new casino and hotel. I'll be gone for the next five days. You gonna miss me a little while I'm gone?

I'll live.

Good night, beautiful.

Good night.

Chapter 12

Tiffani pulled the roasting pan out of the oven and set the turkey on the island next to the ham. Everything was officially ready for Thanksgiving dinner. KJ, who was overly excited, had assisted her in setting the table last night and had helped place the pineapples on the ham. Her guests were arriving at three for a four o'clock dinner. She had a couple of hours to shower and relax. Her eyes continued to glance at her cell phone. She hadn't heard from Broderick since he'd told her he was going to Arkansas. She figured he was back in town, but she wasn't sure if he was coming to dinner. Since their heated argument followed by the rendezvous in her office, they hadn't spoken, which, in a way, was how she'd imagined her "be in the moment" relationship would be. However, now she missed him. Plus, she'd feel awful if he was all alone. That was why she'd invited him in the first place.

Taking a deep breath, she picked up the phone and pressed his name on the screen.

"Hey, Tiff," Broderick answered on the third ring. "Happy Thanksgiving."

"Happy Thanksgiving to you. Are you back in town?"

"Yep. Got back last night. I was going to call you, but it was late."

"No problem. Whatcha doing?"

"Nothing. Just getting ready to watch the game."

"Oh yeah. I'm sure KJ is somewhere doing that. Um…so are you…"

"Mom," KJ yelled out.

"Hold on. KJ is calling me." She exited the kitchen and walked out into the living room. "What's wrong?"

"It's freezing all of sudden." He rubbed his hands together.

"It is chilly in here. I've been in the hot kitchen all day. Turn the heat up."

"I did, Mom. It's on eighty degrees, but it's blowing out cold air. It's only warm upstairs."

Tiffani walked around to all of the downstairs vents and placed her hand over them. The air was indeed cold. Each floor had its own heating unit and because the lower level wasn't open-plan concept, the upstairs heat didn't travel downstairs.

"Great, the downstairs heat isn't working. I'll go

to the basement and check the furnace. Go put on a sweater." She slapped her hand on her forehead when she remembered she was still on the phone. "Broderick, are you there?"

"Yep. Did you forget to pay the gas bill?" he joked.

"Not funny. I paid it. I don't know why the heat isn't working. I just changed the filter a few weeks ago."

"When was the last time you had it serviced?"

Her face scrunched into a frown. "Um…never, I believe." She sat on the bottom step in the basement and hugged her arms around herself. It was even colder down there.

"Is there a fireplace in your dining room?"

"No. I don't have fireplaces in every room like you do. Only the family room and my bedroom. I guess I could move the dining room table in there, but the TV is in that room and the men wanted to watch the game." Frustrated, she raked her hands in her hair and plopped her head on her knees.

"Tell you what. Just have your family come over here."

Stunned, she lifted her head as she actually contemplated his offer. "Broderick…we can't."

"Why not? I have plenty of china, serving platters and utensils and a huge kitchen. Besides, I've never had a Thanksgiving dinner here. It could be fun. And maybe you'll stop being mad me."

"I'm not mad at you." *Where the heck did that come from?* She was still upset. *Right?*

"Oh, so you do realize that I was telling the truth?"

Exhaling, she hated to admit the actual truth. So instead, she avoided the question.

"Thank you so much for the offer. That's very nice of you, Broderick. I was originally calling you to make sure you were still coming to dinner. I would've hated if you were alone today."

"I know. You're a beautiful and loving person, Tiffani. Call your family and give them my address. I'll see you soon."

"Thank you for this and for the compliment."

"You're welcome, sweetheart."

After calling Megan first, who offered to call everyone else so Tiffani could get ready to leave, she and KJ made it to Broderick's mansion an hour later. The gate was already open and she parked by the kitchen door so she could carry in the meats. However, Broderick was waiting at the threshold to assist and suggested she and KJ go inside to get out of the cold.

"Wow, Mom. This kitchen is huge." He turned around with his arms stretched out wide.

"Keith, put your arms down and stopping spinning before you get dizzy and break something."

"Yes, ma'am." He took his jacket off and handed it to her.

"Do I have to take my shoes off, too, like I do at Auntie Megan's home?"

"Yes, take your things and hang them in the mudroom we just walked through."

"Hey, sport," Broderick said, strolling in with the box and setting it on the island. "Mom giving you a hard time?"

"Yeah," KJ answered, walking back to the mudroom.

"So, I want to show you the room where Matilda stores all the serving stuff and whatnot."

"That's okay. I brought paper plates that look like real plates and other paper goods. They're in the trunk."

"Nonsense. This is our first Thanksgiving, and we're using real everything."

She tilted her head and twisted her lips to the side. Did he say *our* first Thanksgiving? She shrugged it off as she and KJ—who'd caught up with them—walked to a room off from the kitchen that contained shelves of china, glasses and serving platters and other entertainment items.

"Oh my goodness." Her eyes widened at all of the gorgeous items. It looked as if she was in a mini Waterford or Mikasa warehouse. "Broderick, these things are too beautiful to use."

"I like those plates," KJ said, pointing to a set of china behind a glass case.

"Don't touch anything, KJ." She walked over to the set he had his eye on and gasped. "It's Antique Lace by Mikasa," she said quietly. It was the china she'd originally registered for, but when she'd shown it to Keith he'd hated it and told her to change to something more unisex. She'd been surprised because she thought men didn't care about such things.

"Not sure what it's called, but when I saw it in a catalog I thought it would be something my mother would like." He shrugged, opened the case and handed Tiffani the plate. "Do you own it, as well?"

"No, no. It's my favorite, though."

"Perfect. We'll use them. KJ, let's finish picking out some glasses, utensils and napkins and then we'll set the table. My staff is off until Monday so you can be my helper."

"Cool."

"KJ, please don't break anything," Tiffani said sternly.

"I won't. Me and Mr. H. got this."

Broderick patted KJ's shoulder. "He'll be fine. I promise. The serving bowls and platters that Matilda likes to use are in the butler's pantry between the kitchen and the smaller dining room, which we'll use today. If you need anything else just call me."

"Okay." She left the guys to set the table and retreated to the kitchen to start cutting up the meats.

A few hours later, the Chase and Monroe crew were seated around Broderick's dining room table. Tiffani couldn't believe that her family was actually there. First of all, she didn't want anyone to think that she and Broderick were a couple because they weren't. Yet they were being cordial and friendly with one another, almost like an old married couple. It felt odd to sit at the head of the table, but when KJ had grabbed her hand he led her to it, and pulled out the chair. When she'd sat down, she'd stared straight ahead into Broderick's penetrating gaze at the other end of the table. A sneering grin had pulled up his left jaw followed by a wink.

After Braxton blessed the food, everyone dug in. Tiffani couldn't help but glance every blue moon at Broderick, who was talking to Bryce and Steven about attending a golf tournament in the spring. Preston chatted with KJ about a few more video games he wanted him to test out. And the twins discussed their parents' upcoming wedding anniversary dinner.

"Mom? Can we go around the table and say why we're thankful? My teacher suggested it."

"Is that okay with everyone?" Tiffani asked, hoping they'd entertain his request.

"Great idea, KJ," Braxton answered.

"You start, Uncle Braxton, and we can go around the table and end with Mommy."

"Sure. I'm thankful that I'm here with my family for dinner this year. Between running the club and going on tour, I don't get to see you all as much as I would like to and I feel very blessed to be here now. Unfortunately, I have to leave in an hour because Café Love Jones is open tonight. Um... Steven you're next."

"I promise to be brief. I'm truly thankful I'm here with all of you on this special occasion and that I'm home with my lovely wife, Megan. I hate leaving when Congress is session, but I love coming home to you." Steven leaned over and kissed his wife's cheek. "Your turn, baby."

"Well, I'm thankful to announce that KJ will no longer be the only Chase child. We're pregnant with twins!"

Tiffani and Sydney screamed and got up to hug Megan as the men shook hands with Steven. Broderick stepped out and returned with a cigar for Steven. After everyone settled down it was Sydney's turn.

"Wow, I'm thankful I'm going to be an auntie to twins and I'm truly thankful that I'm not stressed at work anymore. I happily leave the GBI headquarters every day at five o'clock to race home to my hunk of a man. You're next, counselor," Sydney said to Bryce.

"First of all, I'm grateful for my gorgeous wife rushing home to me and I'm grateful my law practice is flourishing. Best decision I ever made, next to marrying Syd, of course. It's on you, Broderick."

Broderick was quiet for a moment as if he were contemplating. Tiffani gave him a sweet smile and a wink to encourage him.

"Wow, I have a lot to be thankful for, especially lately." His eyes rested on Tiffani. "I'm thankful that my father and I finally have decided to take a leap and mend our relationship. I'm so grateful to Tiffani for encouraging me to do so. She's been a true angel since she's entered my life. Even though I know she doesn't trust me at the moment because of some business-related issues, I truly hope that one day she realizes just how much I hate that she's hurting. And I'm thankful for KJ for giving me a cool nickname."

"Thanks, Mr. H."

Everyone laughed, except for Tiffani, who sat frozen in her seat.

Broderick glanced to his left. "Preston, I believe you're next."

"I'm thankful to be here among family and new friends. Broderick, it's very commendable of you to open up your home to our family at the last minute, and even though my sister is still on the fence, I like you so if she takes you back, don't mess up."

Broderick sipped his wine and glanced at Tiffani, who was flushed with nervousness. "I'll keep that in mind, Preston. KJ I believe you're next, young man."

"I'm thankful for Mommy taking care of me without my father. I'm thankful for both my grandparents, for all of you, my teacher and the fact that my class won the reading bowl."

"That's very sweet, KJ." Tiffani paused as the cotton on her tongue thickened. Broderick hadn't taken his eyes off of her the entire dinner. She was sure he was going to soak in every single word she was about to say. "I'm thankful for a lot of things in my life right now. My KJ and all of you. My bakery is doing quite well, and even though I'm not sure what is happening with the shopping center in the near future, I'm fortunate my dream of owning a bakery came true this year. I'm thankful that at the last minute Broderick offered his home to us for dinner because I was a nervous wreck when I realized the heat wasn't working right before everyone was scheduled to arrive. But he saved the day and for that I'm grateful to him and the special friendship that we have. Cheers." She raised her wineglass in the air and everyone else followed suit. There was so much more she wanted and needed to say to Broderick, but for now she simply wanted him to know how much she appreciated him.

After dinner, Preston volunteered to help Tiffani wash dishes while the other men retreated to the study to smoke cigars, except for Braxton, who had left right after dinner.

"You sure you don't want to hang with the menfolk?" Tiffani asked, passing her brother a plate to dry.

"Nah, I don't smoke cigars or care much about politics. No offense to Steven, of course."

"I thought you were bringing Kay or the chick from Phipps Plaza or some other girl."

"I had a Thanksgiving brunch with this one girl, and I'm meeting the chick from Phipps around nine for a movie. We're checking out that new action flick with your favorite actor and then back to my loft for a little dessert."

"Geez. How many women are you juggling?"

"Enough. How's your artsy friend, Blythe?"

Tiffani set the last wineglass in the drying rack and snickered. "Not thinking about you."

"She was checking me out. I know women." He stacked the last plate, then picked all of them up. "Show me where these go and then I have to jet."

"Follow me."

After her brother left, the others bid their goodbyes, as well. KJ was hanging out in the media room and Tiffani decided it was late and it was time for them to go, too. She found Broderick in the library sipping on a drink and smoking his cigar on the couch.

"Come sit with me, beautiful. You look exhausted."

She crashed next to him and closed her eyes for a moment. "I am. Thank you so much for your hospitality today. My family and I truly appreciate it, considering you didn't have to and we're barely speaking."

"Correction, you're barely speaking because you don't want to enter into a real relationship again, even though I keep telling you I'm not him. I get it. You're scared but you can't keep using the excuse of me betraying you because you think I was aware of something that I wasn't. Deep down you know I'm telling the truth. Granted, maybe you didn't realize it at first, but you know the kind of man I am. I have no reason to lie to you, and I pulled out of the deal because I would never want to hurt you, angel."

She swiped her hands through her hair and looked away from him because he was right. She was scared. At one point, she'd thought Keith was perfect, until he made her feel lower than the Georgia red clay on the bottom of her shoes. She feared taking that chance again.

"Broderick I just need more time," she said quietly. "But I do believe that you are telling the truth about not knowing and I appreciate you for pulling out of the deal."

"Well, I may have pulled out from the group but my partners and others have not. I've been keeping up with it and Harvey is looking to sell before the end of the year. I don't know who he's leaning toward but my bet would be whoever offers the most, and that's more than likely the ones who want to expand. Either way, your lease would be safe until it's up. I would suggest searching for a new location in the meantime just to be prepared."

She yawned wide and stood, stretching her arms out. "I better get going before I can't drive me and my baby home."

"Stay here. I have plenty of rooms. Besides, you have no heat, and KJ is having a blast playing video games on the big screen."

"The heat upstairs works fine. I'll call you when we get home. It's only a thirty-minute drive."

"All right." He pulled her into his arms and kissed her forehead tenderly. She thought he was going to move his lips lower, but he didn't. A part of her was disappointed for a moment, but she knew he was respecting her wishes.

As she lay in bed that night, Tiffani knew she needed to make a decision before she lost a good man that loved and cherished her. Broderick was patient and kind. Even in the beginning Keith had been none of those things. He was high strung, impatient and clingy, which she thought was cute at first until she realized he wasn't being clingy—he was being territorial and controlling. However, she'd married him anyway, thinking perhaps he'd tone down. But it had only gotten worse. And although Broderick hadn't mentioned the word *marriage*, he had mentioned forever to her, and that was the same thing. As she drifted off to sleep, she prayed she would make the best decision for her and for KJ.

Chapter 13

Tiffani placed a half dozen peach bear claws into a box for a customer and smiled sweetly even though deep down she was a nervous wreck. It was the week after Thanksgiving and she'd barely seen Broderick since dinner at his home. He was back and forth between Arkansas negotiating the details of the casino and North Carolina for the groundbreaking ceremony. He'd stopped by the bakery that morning for a quick coffee and Danish break before he'd jetted back to North Carolina for a meeting with Devin and all of the investors of the lakefront subdivision.

Retreating to the kitchen, she checked on the Christmas cookies and cupcakes she was baking for the next day. A woman's screaming from the front jolted her out the door to see Blythe running toward her as if she'd just won the lottery.

Blythe grabbed her hands and began jumping up and down. She was trying to speak, but she was out of breath. Tiffani pulled her into the kitchen because a few customers were watching intently.

"Calm down and tell me what's going on. Did you finally break the drought that you keep calling celibacy?" Tiffani was joking; she knew Blythe was serious about staying celibate until she found the one.

Blythe rolled her eyes. "No. Better. Someone bought the plaza this morning and they aren't expanding it."

Tiffani's eyes widened. She almost jumped up and down but stopped herself. "Before I start doing the happy dance with you, tell me everything you know."

"The chick over at the used bookstore said Harvey sold it to the highest bidder and it was a sole person, not an investment group."

Tiffani screamed at the top of her lungs. "That's wonderful. Who bought it?"

"The person wants to remain anonymous, but whoever he or she is must have a lot of money to outbid the investment groups. You know they really wanted to expand. This is prime real estate."

"And are you sure the new owner doesn't want to tear the place down and raise leases?"

"Nope, just some cosmetic stuff that we all know is needed. There's some marketing team that's going to come in and assist the individual stores with marketing strategies at no cost to us. Now are you going to do the happy dance with me?"

Tiffani grabbed her hands and started the happy dance all over again, ending it with a hug. "This is wonderful news. I can't wait to tell Broderick."

"Uh-huh." Blythe crossed her arms over her chest. "So it's safe to say you two are back together?"

Tiffani sighed and shrugged. "I don't know what we are, but I just know I don't want to be without him. I'm in love with him, and I need to own up to that." Tiffani exhaled in relief that she'd had the aha moment Megan had mentioned would eventually come. There was no turning back. It was out in the universe and now she would deal with it which included telling him as soon as possible.

"Then that's all that matters. I have to go back to work. Go call your man."

Tiffani rushed back to her office and called Broderick, but it went straight to voice mail, which had stated his box was full. She decided to send a text message for him to call her whenever he had a chance. She made a few more phone calls to her parents, Preston and Megan.

Megan called her back a few minutes later. "I just received your message and that's exciting, news, Tiffy. Have you spoken to Broderick?"

"No. He's out of town and his voice mail is full. Besides, I'd rather tell him in person."

"No, that's not what I meant. I'm here in North Carolina and Broderick had to fly back to Atlanta about an hour ago. He got a phone call saying his father was being rushed to Emory Hospital. I think he had a heart attack or a stroke."

"Oh no! That's terrible. I'll go out there now. Thanks, Megan."

After calling her parents to pick up KJ for her and making sure that Kendall and Mindy were fine with running the bakery for a few hours, she filled a box with assorted treats for Broderick and headed out to the hospital. She'd tried calling him, but he didn't answer.

Once learning what floor and room Roderick Hollingsworth was on, she made it up there and peeked in, but it was empty. Walking around the corner to the nurse's station, she spotted Broderick in the waiting room staring up at the TV and watching the news.

"Broderick," she called out and made her way over to him.

Shocked, he rose and gave her a warm hug. "How did you know I was here?"

"Megan told me your dad had a heart attack. I've been trying to call you."

"I'm not getting any reception in the hospital." He held up his cell phone and pointed to the lack of bars.

"How's your father?" she asked. She'd hate for something to happen now that the two men were becoming close. Broderick was finally receiving the love from his father that he had always needed in his life.

"Well, he didn't have a heart attack. It was just indigestion, but his blood pressure is a bit high so they're doing tests on everything else. What brings you here?"

"I came to check on you. I didn't want you here alone."

His face softened. "That's so sweet," he said, running his hand down the front of her hair. "What's in the box?"

She handed it to him as they sat down next to each other. "Snacks and some stuffed croissant sandwiches. I was experimenting today."

He leaned over in her ear and whispered, "Nothing wrong with experimenting."

She rolled her eyes and smiled. "You're so bad, Broderick."

"No, bad would be taking you into one these empty rooms and making love to you. I think I spotted one on the way up."

Her skin flushed at the thought. She missed his kisses and sensual caresses. She decided to tell him her news before she dragged him into one of the empty rooms herself.

"I have good news to share."

He glanced up from digging around in the box and pulled out a macaroon. "What's that?" he asked, not looking directly at her.

"Someone bought Premium Village today, and they're not changing anything except for some updates. But no lease increase."

"Do you know who bought it?" he asked nonchalantly, biting into the macaroon.

"No name. Just that it's an individual who prefers to remain anonymous. Do you think you could find out since that's your circle?"

He shrugged. "I don't know, but I'm glad everything worked out for you."

"Me, too. Blythe and I figured it had to be someone with a lot of money to outbid the investment groups, especially those who wanted to expand."

He simply nodded. "Pass me one of those croissant thingies."

"Let me know what you think."

He bit into it and bobbed his head. "This is good. Turkey, cheese and spinach. You should definitely add this to the menu. Serve it for lunch with some chips or something. Drive a little more business your way. For the record, I did take Marketing 101."

She playfully pinched his cheek at his remark. "That's what I was thinking. Now that I don't have to move, I can think straight again." She wrapped her hands around his biceps and rested her head on his shoulder. He kissed her forehead, and she exhaled with a smile.

"I'm glad you came," he said, placing another tender kiss to her forehead. "Thank you."

"Of course. I love you. Where else would I be?" As soon as she said the words, she froze. She didn't know what had come over her. She'd just blurted it out so naturally, but she meant it. She sat up and looked at his handsome face, which was currently in a state of shock.

"Say it again, beautiful."

She laughed. "I love you, Broderick. Very much."

"I love you too, Tiffani. There's nothing I wouldn't do to make you happy." He lifted her chin and kissed her gently. "I better stop before I really go search for an empty room."

"You're funny. If this investing thing doesn't work out you can always take your act on the road," she teased, returning his kiss.

"I think it's safe to say I'm good at what I do. I told you I can retire tomorrow with no money worries."

"Mmm…" She stopped and tilted her head to the side. "Broderick, did you…no…wait… Did you?"

"Did I what, babe?" he asked with a slightly raised eyebrow.

"You bought the plaza, didn't you?" She turned her body toward him as her breathing became stifled in her throat while she waited for the answer she knew. It was written all over his face.

"Yes."

She put her hands over her mouth as the tears welled up in her eyes. "I can't… I thought…" Tiffani sat back in her chair and then turned toward him once again. She couldn't keep still. He drew her onto his lap and rubbed her back tenderly.

"Breathe, baby. Yes. I bought it. What gave it away?"

"You mentioned the driving more business my way

along with marketing, and Blythe told me that the new owner wanted to bring in a marketing team. Only you would think of something like that. Plus, you had a meeting this morning nearby, and not too long after Blythe rushed in with the news."

"Well, I take it you're happy with my purchase."

"Ecstatic, but I thought you weren't interested in buying the plaza."

"I wasn't. I bought it for you."

"For me?"

"Babe, the bidding was really close. If it had gone the other way, you'd definitely have to start searching for a new place. I couldn't have you unhappy. You've worked hard to make your dream come true. Plus, since we've been together you've never asked me for anything. Most women I date want trips to Paris, shopping sprees, expensive bags and shoes. You just wanted to be with me…except when you were mad at me. And most important, no one since my mother has showed me so much love and concern as you. Even when you weren't speaking to me, you still encouraged me to go see my father and now he and I are working on our relationship." He paused, taking her hands in his. "Look where you are right now. You're by my side at the hospital because you said you didn't want me to be alone. Plus, you brought food. I believe you're a keeper." He kissed her hands and followed it with a deep kiss on the lips.

She placed her palms on his cheeks to stop herself from seducing him right there in the waiting room. "I'm speechless. I can't believe you bought it. Wait, so now you're my landlord?"

"No, I'll have someone at BJH Corp run it. I have some ideas and some cosmetic changes that need to be made."

"I'll be more than happy to write you a list."

"I know you're being sarcastic, but I actually do want the store owners' opinions. We'll have a meeting after the holidays."

"Broderick…you're something else, you know that?"

He grinned and pinched her butt. "No, you were when you said I love you. Baby, that was the best three words I've heard in a long time and I'm glad they came from you. I fell in love with you when I saw you walk down that aisle. I had imagined me standing up there and that you were walking toward me. And just so we're clear, I know you aren't up to remarrying just yet, so I won't pressure you. Knowing you love me the way you do is perfect, beautiful."

Tiffani lowered her lips to his and kissed him with all the love and passion she had for him. "Mmm…baby, I love you so much, and I wouldn't mind a little pressure. I *will* marry you whenever you ask me. You'll just need to get permission from KJ."

Broderick ran his hands in her thick tresses and pulled her to him as he gently nibbled her bottom lip. A soft sigh arose from her throat. "I'll definitely ask KJ first. I have a feeling he'd want to have a talk with me."

Tiffani giggled and scooted off his lap and back on

to her chair when she saw an older couple walk into the waiting area. "Yes, he'll probably want to talk to you."

"Young lady, you could've stayed on your man's lap," the older lady said as she sat across from them with her husband. "Girl, if Bill's knees weren't so bad I'd be sitting on his lap right now!"

Broderick and Tiffani laughed as Bill patted his knees. "You can come sit on me, Hazel. I don't mind. Been with my wife for almost fifty years now. Just have to rub some muscle relaxer on me afterward."

"Congratulations on fifty years," Tiffani stated. "That's a wonderful accomplishment."

"And we will get there." Broderick leaned over and kissed her cheek just as the doctor walked in to see him. Broderick stood and strode to the door. "How's my old man?"

"Your father is fine. His blood pressure was up a tad because he'd forgotten to take the medication. Blood work is good and he is free to go. He's back in the room gathering his belongings."

Broderick shook his hand. "Thank you, Dr. Watson."

Moments later, Broderick and Tiffani arrived at his dad's room. He was sitting on the bed dressed in jeans and a sweater and watching a sports show. Tiffani couldn't believe just how much the two men looked and even sat alike. They may not have been in each other's lives much, but they sure had the same mannerisms and facial expressions.

"Dad, you're all set."

Rod noticed them for the first time and muted the television. "I'm ready, son. And who's this beautiful young woman?"

"This is Tiffani Chase, my girlfriend. Tiffani, this is my father, Roderick Hollingsworth."

Standing, Rod held out his hand and Tiffani shook it. "You know my son is crazy about you. I'm glad he's found a good woman who truly loves him."

"It's nice to meet you, Mr. Hollingsworth, and I do love him very much."

"That's what I want to hear." He turned to Broderick. "Even more beautiful in person. Now let's go. I've been in this hospital long enough."

Later on that evening, Tiffani lay nestled in Broderick's arms in his bed. They'd just made love slow and sensually. She was still coming down from her high as he held her against his rigid chest as if he were protecting her from the cold weather. She was at peace; she'd never known love could be this serene. Tiffani snuggled her head closer in his neck as he slept soundly. Running her fingers along his skin she relished in its warmth and smoothness. She breathed in his masculine aroma along with the fresh scent of sweat from their sensual lovemaking session. She was elated she'd found the one man who could make her change her mind about being in a real relationship. He was perfect in every way, and she loved the special bond and connection that they shared.

Kissing his neck, she whispered. "I love you, Broderick."

He grinned sleepily. "And I love you. Now come here and give me the sweetest kiss, just like the first one that made me fall in love with you."

And she happily obliged him.

Epilogue

Tiffani squinted her eyes as the boat pulled ashore to Broderick's private island in the Keys. He'd sent her on a shopping excursion with his black card and an assistant to shop in Miami while he and KJ prepared a surprise. KJ had been hinting at lobsters from Maine, so she figured the guys were making dinner for her. In the five months they'd been together, Broderick and KJ had been getting along like father and son. She was truly happy about that as well as her own relationship with Broderick.

However, now her curiosity was getting the best of her because there were extra boats and staff on the island. When she'd left, there were no staff present and hadn't been that entire week. Once the boat was docked, she saw KJ running toward her in a tuxedo on the boardwalk along with the four-month-old Weimaraner puppy, Muhammad Ali, she'd given to him for his ninth birthday.

"Mom, come see your surprise." He pulled her along until they reached the front of the beach house, with Ali running alongside. She was astonished to see her entire family standing in a circle lit with candles and rose petals scattered about. Broderick stood in the middle wearing a tuxedo and holding out his hand to her. She took it and a nervous quiver shook through her.

"Baby, what's going on?" she asked as tears began falling and clouding her vision.

He squeezed her hand in his and used the other to take his handkerchief out and dry her tears. "I wanted to do something special for you, so I invited your entire family. Your parents, your grandmother, Preston, the rest of the Chases and even your family from Memphis. My dad, Ms. Dottie and Blythe are here, too. The only person who isn't here is my mother, but I know that she's smiling on us. If she were here she'd adore you just like I do."

He cleared his throat before continuing. "I needed all of them here because I wanted them all to know just how much I love you and that I will honor you and cherish you to the end of my days, my love. You have brought so much love and joy to me, and KJ has, too. Before you, I was just a man all about business and making more money. However, having you in my life has shown and taught me to slow down and enjoy the people around me, especially you and KJ and, of course, my dad."

She tried to speak but couldn't as she listened to his words. She ran her hand along his beard. "Broderick... what are..." The happy tears in her throat were clogging her vocal cords. She patted his chest and looked up at the man who truly loved her.

"Beautiful, I love you. You will never, ever have to worry about me wanting to control you or taking away your independence. Your drive and ambition and your love and concern for others are what attracted me to you. You're beautiful inside and out."

He paused as he settled on one knee. Tiffani shrieked. In the background, she heard all of the females in the circle, especially Megan who was now seven months pregnant, scream and cheer, as well.

"First of all, before I was allowed to get on one knee, I had a serious man-to-man talk with KJ to make sure he wanted me to be a part of both of your lives forever." Broderick looked at KJ, who was standing next to his mother. "And what did you say, son?"

Tiffani smiled down at her handsome son and held his hand in her free one as tears ran down her cheeks.

"I said that I love my mom and I know she's happy with Mr. H. He has my permission to ask you something. However, I also told him that I know karate and if he ever speaks to you the way my father used to he would have to answer to me."

Tiffani stooped down and kissed her son's cheek. He stepped back and stood with his grandfather. Tiffani turned back to Broderick and nodded. She was still too choked up to speak.

"My beautiful Tiffani Serena Chase, you already know I've loved you since the second I laid eyes on you. Couldn't help it. You stir something in me so deep that no one ever has before, and I want to spend the rest of my life showing you just how much I love you. Will you please marry me, Tiffani?" He pulled a Tiffany & Co. ring box out of his tuxedo coat pocket and opened it.

Tiffani was speechless. She couldn't believe that she'd found a man she could finally open her heart up to and let in without any fears or regrets. He truly loved her and KJ. She knew that Broderick would never treat her than anything less than an equal partner and helpmate. She'd finally found her soul mate.

"Yes, I'll marry you Broderick Jerold Hollingsworth. I can't wait to spend my life with you."

Everyone cheered as Broderick slipped the five-carat pink diamond on her ring finger. He stood, gathered her in his arms and kissed her passionately. He twirled her around while she laughed and cried. Once he set her back on her feet, she looked around truly for the first time and noticed everyone was dressed in after-five attire except for her.

"Everyone is dressed up but me." She stared down at her sundress.

Broderick smiled. "You are so right, my dear, and

since this is our engagement party, you should be dressed up, too. I believe your friend Elle Lauren sent you something to wear. Why don't you go look in our bedroom?"

Tiffani wrinkled her forehead in confusion. "Elle sent something? She only designs wedding attire."

"Well, she didn't send a wedding gown. It's pink and very beautiful. Why, do you want to get married right now?" A wide grin crossed his face, and she reached up and kissed him.

"Yes, don't you?" she asked matter-of-factly.

"Yes, very much so. In fact, we have an ordained minister here, and since everyone we know and love is here, we can." Broderick drew her in his arms and kissed her softly on the lips.

"Who's the ordained minister?" She looked around at everyone she was related to, knowing none of them was ordained.

"I called him in just in case."

Tiffani laughed and kissed him again. "I love you, and I'm going to run and put on my gown so I can be your wife as soon as possible." She turned to her mom, who had tears in her eyes. She kissed her mother's cheek. "Mom, will help me get dressed? And Dad, I know it's your job, but you gave me away once before. Can KJ do it this time?"

"That's fine with me, darling." He kissed her forehead before she turned to Preston, kissed his cheek and rustled his hair.

"Love you, baby sis. For the record, Broderick and I had a talk, as well."

"I'm not surprised." She hugged him tightly. "I love you, too."

Her eyes scanned the crowd. "Braxton, think you can play at this impromptu wedding? There's a baby grand in the living room just waiting for you."

"I will play whatever you want."

"All righty. We're all set. I'll be back."

An hour later, they were all toasting champagne to the newlyweds. Tiffani was elated as she stood with Broderick, his arms wrapped around her waist. She felt safe with him in every aspect. She knew he would take their vows seriously, especially because he had shed a few tears as she walked down the aisle to him.

Later on that night, when everyone left to go back to their hotel in Key West, the newlyweds lay on the hammock after their first session of making love as husband and wife.

Broderick rubbed her back tenderly and kissed her forehead every now and then. "It's so peaceful out here. It was the perfect place to get married."

"I agree. The first task when we return to Atlanta is to apply for a marriage license and get married again, to make it legal."

"We'll go first thing Monday morning. I can't wait to marry you all over again, beautiful."

"Then I can finally change my last name."

"That's right, Mrs. Hollingsworth, or is it Mrs. Chase-Hollingsworth?"

"Nope, just Tiffani Hollingsworth. I don't need the Chase. I want to be your wife and want your name only. I think I kept my maiden name for personal reasons the first time because I knew I shouldn't have married him." She kissed her favorite spot on his neck. "I love you. I only want to be Mrs. Hollingsworth. I love the way that sounds." She giggled and kissed his neck again.

"You keep doing that and we'll be back in the bedroom before you know it."

"That's the whole idea, Mr. Hollingsworth."

"I'm going to love the next fifty plus years with you, Mrs. Hollingsworth."

* * * * *

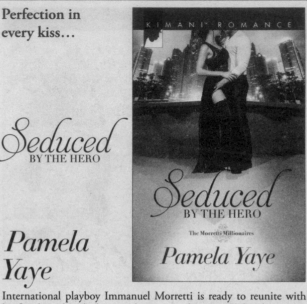

KPNN4281115

REQUEST YOUR FREE BOOKS!

2 FREE NOVELS
PLUS 2 FREE GIFTS!

KIMANI™
ROMANCE

Love's ultimate destination!

KROM15

*When Bailey Westmoreland follows loner Walker Quinn
to his Alaskan ranch to apologize for doing him wrong,
she can't help but stay to nurse the exasperating man's
wounds, putting both their hearts at risk...*

*Read on for a sneak peek at
BREAKING BAILEY'S RULES,
the latest in* New York Times *bestselling author*
Brenda Jackson*'s*
WESTMORELAND series.

Bailey wondered what there was about Walker that was
different from any other man. All it took was the feel of
his hand on her shoulder... His touch affected her in a
way no man's touch had ever affected her before. How did
he have the ability to breach her inner being and remind
her that she was a woman?

Personal relationships weren't her forte. Most of the
guys in these parts were too afraid of her brothers and
cousins to even think of crossing the line, so she'd only
had one lover in her lifetime. And for her it had been
one and done, and executed more out of curiosity than
anything else. She certainly hadn't been driven by any
type of sexual desire like she felt for Walker.

There was this spike of heat that always rolled in her
stomach whenever she was around him, not to mention
a warmth that would settle in the area between her legs.

Even now, just being in the same vehicle with him was making her breasts tingle. Was she imagining things or had his face inched a little closer to hers?

Suggesting they go for a late-night ride might not have been a good idea, after all. "I'm not perfect," she finally said softly.

"No one is perfect," he responded huskily.

Bailey drew in a sharp breath when he reached up and rubbed a finger across her cheek. She fought back the slow moan that threatened to slip past her lips. His hand on her shoulder had caused internal havoc, and now his fingers on her face were stirring something to life inside her that she'd never felt before.

She needed to bring an end to this madness. The last thing she wanted was for him to get the wrong idea about the reason she'd brought him here. "I didn't bring you out here for this, Walker," she said. "I don't want you getting the wrong idea."

"Okay, what's the right idea?" he asked, leaning in even closer. "Why did you bring me out here?"

Nervously, she licked her lips. He was still rubbing a finger across her cheek. "To apologize."

He lowered his head and took possession of her mouth.

Don't miss
BREAKING BAILEY'S RULES
by New York Times *bestselling author*
Brenda Jackson, available November 2015 wherever
Harlequin® Desire books and ebooks are sold.

www.Harlequin.com

HDEXP1015